LOVE COMES TO THE CASTLE

Barbara Cartland

Barbara Cartland Ebooks Ltd

This edition © 2021

ISBNs

9781788675376   EPUB

9781788675383   PAPERBACK

Book design by M-Y Books
m-ybooks.co.uk

THE BARBARA CARTLAND ETERNAL COLLECTION

The Barbara Cartland Eternal Collection is the unique opportunity to collect all five hundred of the timeless beautiful romantic novels written by the world's most celebrated and enduring romantic author.

Named the Eternal Collection because Barbara's inspiring stories of pure love, just the same as love itself, the books will be published on the internet at the rate of four titles per month until all five hundred are available.

The Eternal Collection, classic pure romance available worldwide for all time .

THE LATE DAME BARBARA CARTLAND

Barbara Cartland, who sadly died in May 2000 at the grand age of ninety eight, remains one of the world's most famous romantic novelists. With worldwide sales of over one billion, her outstanding 723 books have been translated into thirty six different languages, to be enjoyed by readers of romance globally.

Writing her first book 'Jigsaw' at the age of 21, Barbara became an immediate bestseller. Building upon this initial success, she wrote continuously throughout her life, producing bestsellers for an astonishing 76 years. In addition to Barbara Cartland's legion of fans in the UK and across Europe, her books have always been immensely popular in the USA. In 1976 she achieved the unprecedented feat of having books at numbers 1 & 2 in the prestigious B. Dalton Bookseller bestsellers list.

Although she is often referred to as the 'Queen of Romance', Barbara Cartland also wrote several historical biographies, six autobiographies and numerous theatrical plays as well as books on life, love, health and cookery. Becoming one of Britain's most popular media personalities and dressed in her trademark pink, Barbara spoke on radio and television about social and political issues, as well as making many public appearances.

In 1991 she became a Dame of the Order of the British Empire for her contribution to literature and her work for humanitarian and charitable causes.

Known for her glamour, style, and vitality Barbara Cartland became a legend in her own lifetime. Best remembered for her wonderful romantic novels and loved by millions of readers worldwide, her books remain treasured for their heroic heroes, plucky heroines and traditional values. But above all, it was Barbara Cartland's overriding belief in the positive power of love to help, heal and improve the quality of life for everyone that made her truly unique.

AUTHOR'S NOTE

Priest Holes, Secret Passages and Sinister Dungeons are to be found in most ancient English Castles and many Ancestral Homes.

I remember the first Priest Hole I saw, which was at Madresfield Court, the seat of the Earl Beauchamp. It opened unexpectedly in the centre of the floor where one would never expect to find it.

In a secret room in Longleat, the beautiful house belonging to the Marquis of Bath, the bones of one of his ancestors who had mysteriously been bricked up there centuries ago were found when workmen were making alterations to the house.

Today, children still find them fascinating and redolent with history and it is intriguing to speculate how many lives have been saved by playing what the children now call 'Hide and Seek'.

CHAPTER ONE
1885

'What am I to do?' Jaela asked herself.

She then walked ove the garden of the Villa, which was bright with bougainvillaea and hibiscus blossom. The lilies were just coming into bud and she well remembered how they had been her father's favourite.

At the thought of him she felt that sickening stab in the heart that he was dead.

He had filled her whole life for the last three years and she had no idea now what to do with herself. She had been just seventeen when her mother died and her father, whose health had never been robust, had turned to Jaela to find comfort and support.

She loved being with him for no one had a sharper or more unusual mind.

Lord Compton of Mellor had been one of the most outstanding Lord Chancellors that England had ever produced.

As a Queen's Counsel and then a Judge, his *bons mots*, his brilliant speeches and finally his judgements, had been the delight of the newspapers comment columns.

There was seldom a day passed when he was not referred to in the Press.

While his charm and good humour were the admiration not only of his friends but even of the criminals he sent to prison.

But plagued with ill-health he had retired to the South of Italy, which had been a great loss to his own country but a joy to his wife and daughter.

He had bought the lovely Villa Mimosa that was located by the sea between Naples and Sorrento.

They had been so blissfully happy there with their only daughter, who they had sent off to school in Naples.

No one had expected that Lady Compton would die first, but she had caught one of the pernicious fevers that Naples was plagued with from time to time.

Almost before her husband and her daughter could realise it she was dead.

It was then that Jaela had left school without even consulting her father to be with him all the time in the Villa.

She had discovered from her Headmistress who were the best Tutors of Literature, Music and History and she employed them to come to her instead of her going to them.

It was a very satisfactory arrangement, as her Tutors came early in the morning while her father was still resting.

So Jaela could then spend the rest of the day with him.

He, as she had often told him, was a whole encyclopaedia in himself. In fact Jaela often thought how exceptionally lucky she was to have such a brilliant man to teach her, guide her and undoubtedly inspire her.

"Do you realise, Papa," she had said jokingly, "I shall have to remain an old maid for the rest of my life? For I will never find a husband as brilliant as you."

Her father laughed.

"You will fall in love, my dearest, with your heart and not with your brain!"

"Nonsense!" Jaela argued. "I could never love a man who was stupid or could not talk to me seriously about the same subjects as you do."

"Now you are frightening me," her father exclaimed. "In another year I am going to send you to England to make your curtsey to the Queen and meet young people of your own age."

Jaela did not say anything, but she knew that as long as her father lived she would never leave him.

The doctors had told her privately that he was a very sick man. His heart might give out at any moment and he must never exert himself.

Jaela was quite content to sit beside him on the balcony of their Villa or to walk with him very slowly around the garden in the sunshine.

Despite the doctors' warnings that it might be dangerous, she insisted that, when winter came, on moving across the Mediterranean to Algiers.

There it was warmer and there were no cold treacherous winds in the evenings. These came straight, she knew, from the snow-capped mountains.

They had come back only a month ago to their Villa and she had thought that her father seemed better than he had been for a long time.

Then one morning, when she had least expected it, she went into his bedroom to find him dead.

He had a faint smile on his handsome face.

She felt certain that he had died thinking of her mother and that he was now with her.

'They will be happy,' she told herself, 'but what about me?'

She knew that, if she was sensible, she should go back to England.

Her grandparents were all dead, but there were various aunts and cousins, any of whom would be delighted to chaperone her as a rather belated *debutante*.

But for the moment she was in deep mourning and her father had always laughed at the exaggerated 'crêpe and tears'.

But women followed the example of Queen Victoria and it was what would be expected of her.

Especially as her father had been so important and there had been long obituaries of him in the English newspapers and then the Italians, because he had lived in Italy, had followed suit.

'What am I to do?'

The question was still there as she moved towards the stone fountain.

It was throwing its water high up towards the sky, where it then turned into a thousand tiny rainbows.

If she was to stay here, as she would like to do, she would have to find a chaperone. But she wondered how she could endure what would be banal conversation day after day with a woman.

She was so used to the sparkling wit and wisdom of her father. They had duelled with each other in words and Jaela had argued with him just for the fun of it.

It was so exciting to hear him use every possible verbal means to defeat her.

'Oh, Papa,' her heart cried out silently, 'how could you leave me when were so happy together here?'

She felt the tears come into her eyes, but she forced herself not to cry.

"If there is anything I really dislike," Lord Compton of Mellor had said, "it is a woman who weeps to get her own way, but it is a weapon, my dearest, used invariably by your sex."

"They do it to make a man feel strong and masculine and, of course, very superior," Jaela had replied mockingly.

"That is where you are wrong – " her father began.

And they were off again on one of their fascinating arguments, which usually ended with them both laughing at themselves.

Now there was nobody to laugh with and everything seemed very quiet and silent.

As it was nearly luncheontime, Jaela walked slowly back towards the balcony where her father had always sat.

The sunshine immediately turned her hair to gold.

It was not the soft gold of an English sun but the deep burnished gold that Botticelli had painted on Simonetta's head.

It had been the despair of the dyemakers ever since.

It seemed almost to burn in the sunshine and to make Jaela's skin dazzlingly white.

Her eyes, which were the blue of the Mediterranean in a storm, filled her whole face.

"I cannot think where you get your eyes from," her father had often said. "Your mother's were the blue of the sky and so I thought when I first saw them that nothing could be more beautiful."

"And yours are grey, Papa," Jaela said, "and when you are angry they are almost black!"

Her father had laughed.

"I suppose that is true but your eyes are a very strange colour, my dearest girl. It would require a better poet than I am to describe them."

Jaela knew what he was trying to say when she examined her eyes more closely than she had before.

They were a very deep dark blue and occasionally had a touch of green in them.

When she was angry, she thought that they had almost a purple tinge, although it was difficult to describe it to herself.

Now, as she neared the balcony, the man who was waiting for her thought that it would be impossible for any young woman to look lovelier.

She looked in fact as if she had stepped down from Mount Olympus to mix with human beings.

Jaela had reached the steps leading up to the balcony before she saw him.

"Dr. Pirelli," she exclaimed. "How good to see you."

He held out his hand and asked in good English but with a pronounced accent,

"How are you, my dear?"

"I am all right," Jaela replied, "Only, as you can imagine, missing Papa unbearably."

"I was sure you would be doing that," Dr. Pirelli replied, "and I miss him too. I used to look forward eagerly to my visits here to talk with him and, of course, to see you."

Jaela smiled.

"I think you and Papa had so much to say to each other that you usually forgot my very existence."

Dr. Pirelli laughed.

"That is untrue and you are obviously fishing for compliments."

A servant, who was well used to Dr. Pirelli's visits, brought a bottle of the wine that he always fancied and poured out a glass of it.

Dr. Pirelli took it and seated himself in one of the comfortable chairs.

As the servant withdrew, he said,

"I have a suggestion to make to you, Jaela, which may well surprise you."

"A suggestion?" Jaela asked.

"I have been worrying about you," the doctor said, "and you must realise it is important that you should not stay her alone."

"I have thought of that, but I suppose that I could find a chaperone, although the idea of employing some elderly woman who has nothing better to do is somewhat depressing."

"That is what I thought you would say," Dr. Pirelli replied, "and I think that you ought to return to England."

Jaela sighed, but she did not say anything and he went on,

"As I said, I have a suggestion to make to you that might make the journey less tedious."

Jaela looked at him questioningly and he said,

"I think you have heard me speak of the Contessa di Agnolo."

"Yes, of course I have," Jaela nodded. "She lives in that exquisite Villa not very far from Pompeii that I have always longed to visit."

"Although the Contessa has often asked about you, it is something I would not let you do," Dr. Pirelli went on, "because she has for the last year been suffering from tuberculosis."

"You told Papa about her and he thought it very sad."

"It is a tragedy," Dr. Pirelli said. "She is so young and still very beautiful."

"Is there no hope of a cure?" Jaela enquired.

"I wish there was," he replied, "But both lungs are infected and she is in fact dying."

"I am so sorry," Jaela murmured.

There was a short pause and she was wondering how this concerned her when Dr. Pirelli continued,

"The Contessa has a little daughter of just eight years old and a lovely child with a sweet character to whom naturally she is completely devoted."

"I had no idea that she had a child," Jaela said. "I suppose now she will have to be with her father."

"That is exactly what I was going to tell you," Dr. Pirelli said. "The Contessa wishes to send Lady Katherine, or 'Kathy', as she is always called, back to her father."

Jaela was surprised.

"Are you saying that the Contessa is English and the child is not then the daughter of the Conte di Agnolo,"

"I thought perhaps your father would have told you about the Contessa," Dr. Pirelli said.

"He sometimes referred to the Villa, but I cannot remember him ever saying very much about the Contessa."

"I suppose he thought that it would be a mistake for you to be interested in her," the doctor said almost as if he was speaking to himself.

"Why should it be a mistake?" Jaela enquired.

Dr. Pirelli hesitated as if he was feeling for words and then finally he said,

"The Contessa is actually the wife of the Earl of Halesworth."

Jaela looked at the doctor in some surprise.

"You mean," she said slowly, "that she is not – married to the Conte di Agnolo!"

"Unfortunately not," the doctor affirmed, "but to prevent there being any scandal in the neighbourhood, when the Conte brought her here to his Villa he gave her his own name and people who live here have no idea that the Conte has a wife and family living in Venice!"

"But – you and Papa knew this all the time," Jaela pointed out accusingly.

"Your father, of course, knew the Earl of Halesworth by name and he had heard that his wife had run away from him only a few years after they were married."

"And she took her little girl with her?" Jaela asked.

"The child was two at the time," Dr. Pirelli said, "and she could not bear to leave her behind."

But – did not the Earl protest?" Jaela asked.

"I discussed it once with your father," the doctor replied, "and he said from what he remembered the Earl was a very proud man. Like a great many English aristocrats he would do anything rather than have the family name besmirched by a divorce which, when it is a question of a Peer, would have to go through the House of Lords."

"I see," Jaela said. "So he remained silent when his wife left him, although I should have thought that he would have tried to gain possession of his only child."

The doctor did not speak and after a moment she said,

"I suppose it was not so important as she was a girl. If it had been a question of his son and heir, he would have had him back at once."

"I expect you are right," the doctor said. "At any rate little Kathy is with her mother and I have been extremely worried in case she should catch her mother's complaint, which you are well aware is highly infectious."

"Yes, of course, and that must be a headache for you," Jaela said sympathetically. "And what are you going to do about the little girl now?"

"That is what I am going to tell you," the doctor said. "I have talked it over with the Contessa and she has begged me to ask you, because you are English, to take the child back to England and hand her over to her father."

"She asked for *me*?" Jaela exclaimed. "But I have never met her!"

"She has heard a great deal about you," the doctor replied with a smile. "She has been a lonely woman in many ways these past years, even though the Conte adores her and, if it was possible, he would lay the sun and the moon at her feet."

He made a very Italian gesture with his hands before he added,

"But, of course, at times he has to return to his wife and family and then the Contessa is alone."

"Does she have no friends?"

"It seems an odd thing to say, but the answer is very few," he said. "It was difficult for her to mix with the Italians in case anyone should find out that she and the Conte were not married and the English, if they were of any importance, would have drawn their skirts aside in horror because to them she was a 'Scarlet Woman'!"

"Oh – I understand!" Jaela exclaimed. "I wish Papa could have asked her here so that we could have been kind to her."

"I believe your father was thinking of you," the doctor responded simply.

"And now the Contessa wants me to take her daughter to England."

"What I suggest you do is to come with me after luncheon and speak with the Contessa herself. Then I think you will understand that she is desperately worried about to whom she can entrust, for what will be a long journey, her precious little girl."

"I understand," Jaela said, "and if it is possible, of course, I will accompany the child."

She hesitated before she added,

"The only thing is, I have no wish to go to London while I am still in mourning and have to sit talking about Papa – which will make me want – to cry."

"Then the best thing you can do," the doctor said briskly, "is to occupy your mind with something else, which is certainly what your father would want if he was with you."

"I know that," Jaela said, "and perhaps, when I get to England, I will open our country house, which we closed when we came here and put in charge of caretakers."

"I think that would be a sensible thing to do," the doctor agreed, "at least until you can enter the Social world which, as you know, your father always wanted you to do."

"I am not sure it is what I want to do," Jaela admitted.

"That is the first foolish thing you have said," the doctor replied. "You are young, you are beautiful and the sooner you take your place amongst your own people, as your mother and father planned for you, the better."

He spoke firmly in the way, Jaela thought with amusement, he might have spoken to a reluctant convalescent who was afraid after a long illness of facing the world again.

"I know exactly what you are saying to me, dear Dr. Pirelli and I suppose, like the nasty medicine you gave me when we first met, I shall have to 'take what is good for me'!"

"Of course you will," he agreed, "and so now, if you are generous enough to give me something to eat, I will take you to meet the Contessa."

*

The doctor's comfortable carriage drove through the twisting narrow lanes.

Sitting beside him Jaela thought it was most extraordinary that, living so near to the Villa Agnolo, she had never been there before.

Now she understood why, if she spoke to her father about it, he always seemed to have a very little to say.

She knew that her relations would disapprove violently of any lady who could be called a 'Scarlet Woman'.

As the Italians were renowned gossips, she doubted if a large number of them would not have been aware that the Contessa di Agnolo was living a double life.

When they arrived at the Villa it was even more magnificent than it had seemed in the distance and she could well understand that the Conte had wanted a beautiful setting for the woman he loved.

A servant opened the door dressed in a Livery that was very impressive.

They were led through a hall and along a corridor hung with magnificent pictures.

Then they went into one of the most beautiful sitting rooms that Jaela had ever seen.

Everything was white, the walls, the curtains, the coverings on the furniture and the rugs on the polished floor.

The pictures were by the great Italian Masters and their vivid colours shone like jewels against a velvet setting.

There were huge crystal vases filled with fresh flowers.

Jaela was left alone while the doctor ascertained if his patient was ready to receive them.

She walked round the room and saw glass cases filled with exquisite *objets d'art* which she was sure must be worth a small fortune.

She did not have long to look at everything for the doctor returned and he was smiling.

"The Contessa is delighted that you have come to meet her as she hoped you would," he said, "but she is very weak and you must not stay long."

"I do understand," Jaela replied.

They walked up a wide staircase and the doctor then opened a door.

It was a large room, the same size as the sitting room and, although the sun blinds were down outside, it still seemed to be filled with sunshine.

Lying back against lace-trimmed pillows in a canopied bed hung with curtains both of muslin and of silk was the Contessa.

Even though she was pitiably thin, she was still, Jaela thought, one of the most beautiful women she had ever seen.

Her hair was so fair that it was like the first light of dawn.

Her eyes, however, were fringed with dark lashes and, because she was so ill, seemed too large for her face. They were pale green flecked with gold and very English.

She did not look, as Jaela had expected she would, pale and drawn, but she had a touch of colour in both of her cheeks.

Then she was aware, when she thought about it, that this was part of the terrible disease that was destroying her.

Jaela walked to the bed and a nurse placed a chair for her so that she could sit down close to the Contessa.

The sick woman held out her hand which was little more than skin and bone.

"You have come," she began in a soft voice.

"Yes, I have come," Jaela replied, "and, of course, I will help you in any way I can."

"You are so kind."

There was a little pause, as if she found it difficult to speak, before she continued,

~15~

"Please take Kathy home to her father. It was wrong of me to bring her away with me, but I loved her so much."

The words came jerkily from between her lips and then Jaela ,who was holding her hand, said,

"I can understand that and I will certainly look after Kathy for you."

"He must not be angry with her," the Contessa stipulated.

Jaela realised that she was speaking of her husband and she declared consolingly,

"I am sure that he will be very glad to have his daughter back with him."

The Contessa closed her eyes, but she did not take her hand from Jaela's.

The doctor and the nurse had moved away. In fact Jaela, without looking round, thought that they had left the room.

She waited.

Then the Contessa spoke again,

"I have no regrets for myself. Love is very very wonderful! But Stafford did not love me."

"You have been very happy," Jaela said, "and that is all that matters now."

"Very very happy – " the Contessa then murmured. "But Kathy must not be punished for me."

"No, of course not!" Jaela said hastily.

"Take her back," the Contessa said very slowly. "Teach her to be English and it will be better for her that way."

"I will try, I promise you I will try," Jaela stated firmly.

Looking down at the Contessa, she thought it very pitiful that she should be so ill when she was still so young and so lovely.

Because she wanted her to feel happy, she affirmed again,

"I promise you that I will look after Kathy and take her to her father."

"You are very kind."

The Contessa's words were barely audible and her eyes were closed.

Her hand went limp and Jaela realised that she had not the strength to say anything more.

She rose to her feet.

She said a little prayer in her heart that the Contessa would die without any more pain.

Also that the happiness she had known on earth would not be lost in Heaven.

Then she turned and walked to the end of the room where Dr. Pirelli was waiting for her.

He drew her from the bedroom and, when they were outside in the corridor, he said in a voice that showed that he was deeply moved,

"That was very kind of you, Jaela, and no one could have been more gracious."

"I am so desperately sorry for her," Jaela said. "It is such a waste of life to die when she is so young."

"She has been ecstatically happy," the doctor said, "and perhaps none of us can ask for more."

He spoke emotionally and Jaela remembered that he was a widower.

As they were speaking, they had moved not downstairs but along the corridor, which was also filled with some very fine pictures.

The doctor then opened a door and they went into what Jaela realised was a little girl's nursery.

It was beautifully furnished.

There were toys everywhere, a large dolls' house and a rocking horse like those English children always had and a number of coloured cardboard bricks were scattered over the floor.

A little girl was seated amongst them, while an Italian maid was helping her build a castle.

She looked up as they entered, saw the doctor and, giving a cry of delight, scrambled to her feet.

"Dr. Pirelli!" she cried. "You are here. Have you brought me some more of those nice sweeties?"

"I have a whole box of them waiting for you downstairs in my carriage," the doctor replied, "which I promised you if you were a good girl and did not disturb your Mama."

"I have been very very quiet," Kathy said, "have I not, Giovanna?"

She asked the question in Italian and the maid answered her in the same language.

"You have been very good and very quiet."

"Then the box is waiting for you," the doctor said, "and now I want you to meet a very charming lady who is a friend of mine, Miss Jaela Compton."

Jaela crouched down so that she was the same height as Kathy.

"I have been admiring your dolls' house," she said. "I used to have one when I was your age, but it was much smaller."

"Mine is nice," Kathy said, "but I like my horse best."

"What do you call him?" Jaela asked. "I too had a horse and I rode him before I had a real pony."

Kathy, who was not in the least shy, looked at her with interest and Jaela went on,

"I think if you will come with me to England, as your mother wants you to do, you too will have a real pony of your own."

"I will?" Kathy asked. "That would be so lovely! I have wanted a pony, but Mama said there was no room here for it in the garden. But I did ride when we went across the sea."

"On a horse or on a camel?" Jaela asked.

Kathy laughed.

"Both! The camel was funny, very very funny!"

"I am sure it was and you must tell me all about it. If you would like to come home with me, I will show you the photographs of the horses I had when I was in England."

"I would like that," Kathy smiled.

Jaela looked at the doctor.

There was a question in her eyes and he answered by nodding his head.

He spoke to the maid in Italian, telling her to pack some of Kathy's clothes as quickly as possible.

Then holding Kathy's hand, he took her downstairs with Jaela following.

She realised that the child was very quiet the moment they were outside the nursery and passing her mother's bedroom.

She thought it touching that anyone so young had already learnt to be so considerate.

Only as they reached the hall did Kathy say still in a low voice to the doctor,

"Can I go and see Mama before we go?"

"I think your mother is asleep now," the doctor answered, "but if you would just like to peep in and wave to her and blow her a kiss, you can do that."

"I will be very very quiet and I will blow her lots of kisses because I miss kissing her."

Jaela understood that the child had been forbidden to kiss or touch her mother because it was dangerous. And yet there was nobody else with her except for the servants.

They then went to the doctor's carriage and he presented Kathy with a box of sugared almonds.

"Thank you, thank you!" she enthused.

She put up her face in a very natural gesture to kiss the doctor on the cheek.

She opened the box and offered it to the doctor, who refused, and then to Jaela, who accepted one.

Then Kathy sat in the open carriage eating one after another.

"They are very very good," she said, "but Giovanna says that they will make me fat, so Mama ought to eat some."

"Your mother is too ill to eat sweets," the doctor replied.

"You are taking a very long time to make her well," Kathy remarked.

"I have done my best," the doctor replied as if he was on the defensive.

"It is so dull here without Mama," Kathy said. "I would like to have a little dog to play with, but Uncle Diego says a dog would be a nuisance in the Villa."

"I am sure when you get to England you can have a dog," Jaela suggested hastily.

She saw Kathy's eyes light up and knew that this could be a way by which she could gradually forget her mother.

Jaela had adored her own mother and she knew well that Kathy was going to find it very difficult to adjust herself to a world where she was alone.

It struck her as if for the first time that she and Kathy were different ages but were more or less in the same boat.

They were both of them alone with nothing for the moment to cling on to.

'I am sure that her father will mean a great deal to her,' Jaela told herself consolingly.

Then she wondered if the Earl would be glad to see his daughter back after he had been deprived of her company for six years of her life.

It was a problem she certainly did not wish to face at the moment and she brushed it on one side.

Italians work quickly and in a very short time Giovanna came down the stairs with a case containing some of Kathy's clothes.

She also brought with her a bonnet and coat for the child to travel in.

"Now can I blow kisses to Mama?" Kathy asked the doctor.

"Yes," he answered, "but tell nurse what you want to do."

Kathy jumped out of the carriage and ran back into the Villa.

She was only away for a few minutes and when she returned she had her favourite doll in her arms.

"I should have brought Betsy with me," she said as if she reproached herself, "but now she will enjoy travelling in the carriage."

"I am sure she will," Jaela said, "and I hope you will too."

"I liked driving with Mama," Kathy replied. "She used to tell me stories about the places we passed."

"Then that is something I will do," Jaela nodded.

"Do you know any stories?" Kathy enquired.

"Lots and lots," Jaela replied. "And I shall want you to tell me some as well."

"What about?" Kathy asked.

"About everything!" Jaela answered. "The flowers, the trees, the sea, the sky. In fact, if you think about it, there are stories everywhere we look."

Kathy laughed.

"That is a funny idea and I want you to tell me *all* your stories."

"I will tell you lots of stories while we are going to England," Jaela promised, "and you must tell me all the stories about Italy as you have been living here for longer than I have."

"Fairy Stories?" Kathy queried.

"Fairy Stories, stories about Knights, stories of hobgoblins and stories of little girls who enjoy stories."

Kathy grinned.

The doctor had been giving Giovanna instructions about packing all the rest of Kathy's clothes and now he climbed into the carriage.

"I am taking you home," he said, "then I am coming back to see my patient. Some more trunks will be ready then and I will bring them to you this evening."

"Thank you," Jaela replied, "and now I am looking forward to showing Kathy my Villa, and, of course, the fountain."

"Have you a fountain all of your own?" Kathy asked.

"All my own," Jaela answered, "and there is a special story about where it came from and who made it, besides a Fairy Story of what has been happening while it has been in the Villa."

Kathy gave a little cry of delight and slipped her hand into Jaela's.

"Tell me, *tell me*!" she begged. "Tell me the story now. If you do, I will tell you one before I go to bed."

"That is a bargain," Jaela replied.

She put her arm round the little girl and drew her close.

She thought as she did so that Kathy was surely one of the most engaging and attractive children she had ever seen.

She looked up, met the doctor's eyes and knew that he was smiling his approval.

She felt that he had been apprehensive as to whether she would do what he had asked of her and take Kathy with her to England.

For the first time she wondered if there was something that he had not told her about the whole arrangement.

If there was, it might be a more difficult task than she had anticipated.

CHAPTER TWO

Jaela tucked Kathy up in her bed and then bent down to kiss her goodnight.

To her surprise, the child hesitated.

Then she asked,

"Is it safe to kiss you? I was not allowed – to kiss Mama."

"It is quite safe," Jaela replied, "but only if you want to."

Kathy looked at her and then she said,

"I want to, I want to, you are so very nice and kind and you are going to tell me lovely stories."

She put her arms around Jaela's neck and kissed her on the cheek.

Jaela held her closely and she could not help feeling sad that the little girl had been kept away from her mother.

The Contessa was, she realised, the only person of importance in the child's small life.

She cuddled Kathy and felt her warm little body clinging to her.

She told herself that she would do everything she could on the way to England and make her happy.

When Jaela went downstairs to her lonely dinner she thought of what lay ahead.

She finally decided that it was Fate that was making her leave the Villa when she was still thinking that she would rather stay.

'Kathy and I both have to face a new world,' she murmured to herself, "and I am only praying it will be a happy one for her and perhaps an interesting one for me."

*

The next morning Dr. Pirelli arrived at the Villa early.

He had brought with him several trunks that contained Kathy's clothes besides her most treasured possessions.

Kathy was playing in the garden and running round the fountain, which fascinated her.

The doctor sat down in one of the chairs on the balcony.

There was silence for a moment.

And then Jaela said,

"I love Kathy, Dr. Pirelli, and I will look after her, but I want you to be frank with me and tell me everything you know about her father. I have a feeling, but I may be wrong, that you are keeping something back."

Dr. Pirelli looked at her uncomfortably.

"What I had planned," he said, "was that you should take Kathy to Hale Castle and then forget about her."

Jaela raised her eyebrows.

"As I am the only link with her mother, I think if I did that it would be rather cruel."

The doctor did not speak and Jaela went on,

"Of course her father may welcome her with open arms but I was just thinking last night when I went to bed that, as he has not seen her since she was two years old, he may not be as welcoming as you hope."

"She is only a child," the doctor suggested defensively.

"I suppose that is a great point in her favour," Jaela replied, "but he may be one of those men who do not like children,"

The doctor put his hands together.

"You are making difficulties, Jaela," he commented, "and it is unlike you."

"I still think that you are keeping something from me," Jaela retorted.

There was silence.

And then Dr. Pirelli gave in,

"Very well, if you want the truth, some friends of mine, who are English, told me when I was in Paris three years ago that a rather strange thing happened at Hale Castle."

"I would like to hear about it," Jaela stressed firmly.

The doctor sighed before he went on,

"They did not know that I was treating the wife of the Earl of Halesworth and I merely asked about him casually and out of curiosity."

"And what did they tell you?"

"They told me there had been a lot of gossip about the Earl because of something strange that had happened concerning him."

Jaela was listening intently and the doctor continued,

"They did not actually know the Earl personally but, because he was important and they happened to be staying in the same County, he was talked about."

Jaela was aware that this was inevitable, but she did not interrupt.

"What they told me," the doctor went on, "was that he had been involved with a woman, someone who was young and attractive and a widow. Then, for some unaccountable reason, she disappeared!"

"Disappeared?" Jaela exclaimed.

"No one ever knew what had happened to her and my friends said that the neighbours were whispering amongst themselves that she might have been murdered!"

"It sounds incredible!" Jaela exclaimed. "What actually happened?"

The doctor threw out his hands.

"That is all I know. I carne back to Italy and, of course, I did not tell the Contessa."

"So you don't know the end of the story."

"I think, if you ask me, there is no end," the doctor said. "It only struck me as unpleasant because the Earl is Kathy's father and I have a deep affection for the child."

Jaela was silent for a moment.

Then she said,

"You still think that I should take her to her father?"

"But of course. What I heard was obviously a lot of nonsense and if there had been a trial or even a Police investigation, it would have been in all the newspapers."

"You are quite sure it was not?" Jaela enquired.

The doctor nodded.

"I took the trouble to read an English newspaper, which is published weekly in Italy, for several weeks. There was

~28~

no reference to the Earl of Halesworth, so I imagine what I learnt was just careless gossip."

Jaela rose from her chair and stood looking at Kathy alone in the garden.

She looked very delightful against the iridescent water from the fountain.

She might in her white dress and blue sash be one of the Fairies she liked to hear about but she was, Jaela knew, very like her mother.

"The Contessa must have been very beautiful," she said aloud. "Perhaps the Earl was broken-hearted at losing her."

"If he was," Dr. Pirelli replied, "she was not aware of it. Once, when we were talking together, she said,

"'I never knew happiness until I met Diego. He loved me as a woman, while my English husband treated me as if I was a child whom he found rather tiresome'."

"How old is the Earl?" Jaela asked.

"As a matter of interest, I looked him up in a reference book," Dr. Pirelli answered. "He was twenty-seven when his wife ran away from him so he must now be thirty-three."

"Not so very old," Jaela smiled.

"Except to a very sweet gentle woman who just wanted to be loved," Dr. Pirelli replied.

He sounded very Italian as he said it.

With a little smile Jaela thought how much love meant to the Italians and how volubly they could all express their feelings, but an Englishman was taught from the moment he was born to be restrained and controlled.

He was also shy, if that was the right word, of talking about matters of the heart.

She and her father had often compared the characteristics of the different countries of Europe.

Lord Compton had said,

"The Italians are like children! They cry when they are miserable, they sing when they are happy and their hearts throb with emotion from the moment they rise in the morning until the time they go to bed."

Jaela had laughed and he went on,

"They think constantly of women, while our countrymen, my dearest, think of hunting, shooting and fishing!"

"But you were not like that, Papa," Jaela pointed out.

"Only where your mother was concerned," her father replied. "The moment I saw her, I knew that she was everything I had dreamt of secretly but thought I would never find. When I realised that she loved me, I was the most fortunate man in the whole world."

"That is what I want," Jaela said quietly.

"I can only pray that you will find it," Lord Compton answered. "At the same time, my dearest, I want you to marry a man who will be worthy of your beauty."

Jaela looked at her father accusingly.

"Now you are being a snob," she said. "I know quite well that what you mean is that I would marry a Duke, which is most unlikely or some stiff-necked aristocrat who will never be quite sure if I am good enough for him."

"I have never heard such rubbish in my life!" Lord Compton responded angrily.

Then he realised that his daughter was teasing him and chided her,

"Stop being so very irritating! You know exactly what I do want for you and, of course, I am ambitious. I want to see you sitting among the Peeresses at the Opening of Parliament."

"Oh, Papa, how can you be so ridiculous," Jaela asked. "I have no wish to wear a tiara, to open and close Flower Shows and pat children on the head as I present the prizes at school!"

She paused to say more seriously,

"I want to marry a man who is ambitious and as clever as you are. The Prime Minister, if you like, or else an Ambassador to some very civilised country like France."

"Perhaps you are right," her father then conceded. "With your brains you most certainly would inspire a man to climb the ladder of success. At the same time he might be jealous of you."

Jaela kissed her father, saying,

"He is much more likely to be jealous of you, when I continually quote what you have said and tell him how clever and resourceful you are."

Now she thought for the thousandth time that she would never find anyone to love her as her father had loved her mother.

She was intelligent enough to realise that her brain, which her father had rated so highly, could be an impediment.

Her mother, sweet and wonderful as she was, never attempted to argue with her father or to query any decisions he made.

She just adored him and put herself as she put their life entirely in his hands. Whatever he wanted she was completely content to want it too.

Jaela had often wondered to herself if she could be complacent or so easily satisfied.

Her father had always found that being alive was a challenge and that was what she felt as well.

Now a problem had presented itself and she was determined to solve it.

It was to make sure that Kathy was happy in England.

She asked herself what she should do when she arrived at Hale Castle if she thought that the child would not be happy there with her father.

Would there she wondered be any way by which she could take her to another relation?

She opened her lips to ask the question of the doctor and then decided that he would not know the answer.

It would only make him more worried about the whole scenario than he was already.

She could understand that he had a real affection both for the Contessa and for Kathy.

She knew that he would miss the child when she had left Italy, just as he would miss her mother when she died.

'I must not make things worse for him than they are already,' Jaela decided.

Aloud she said,

"I am glad you told me about the Earl, but I imagine by now that they must have found a good explanation for the missing person."

"That is what I am hoping," Dr. Pirelli said quickly, "And why I did not wish to tell you about it."

"The more I know about the Earl the better," Jaela said. "After all I have to persuade Kathy that she wants to see her father and that he will give her the same happy home that she had with her mother."

"Yes, that is true," the doctor agreed, "and I am sure, my dear, it is something that you will be able to do."

Jaela thought that he was being over-optimistic, but she did not say so.

He then proceeded to tell her what arrangements he was making for the journey.

"Do we have to leave so quickly?" Jaela asked.

"It will make the Contessa happy to know that her daughter is on the way to England," the doctor replied.

He did not say anything more, but Jaela knew that he was also thinking that it would be a mistake for Kathy to know that her mother was dead before she left.

He then said,

"Of course the Contessa will pay all your expenses as well her daughter's."

"There is no reason for her to do that," Jaela said. "I have money of my own."

"I know that," the doctor replied, "but the Contessa is really a very rich woman. She had some money before she married and the Conte, who is an extremely wealthy man, gave her everything she required and a great deal more."

He paused before he continued,

"I saw her Solicitor this morning and he showed me her will. Everything has, of course, been left to Kathy who, even apart from her father, will be a very wealthy young woman."

'That will be nice for her,' Jaela thought to herself.

She was thinking that, if her father did not want her, there would always be relations who would be willing to take her.

Especially as she could pay for herself.

"I am therefore arranging," Dr. Pirelli continued, "that you will have a drawing room coach attached to the train that will take you into France as far as Paris. After that your coach will be attached to another train, which will take you to Calais."

"It sounds very luxurious," Jaela said, knowing if she had been on her own, she would have been quite content with a reserved seat in one of the carriages.

"I do want you both to be comfortable," the doctor said simply. "The Courier who will travel with you and make all the necessary arrangements is a very experienced man. He has been to England several times."

"I am very grateful," Jaela said, "And are you or am I writing to the Earl to say that we are arriving?"

To her considerable surprise the doctor did not answer at once and she saw that there was a frown between his eyes.

She waited until finally he answered her,

"I have thought this over very carefully and I think it would be a mistake to do anything before you get there."

"Do you really mean that we should just turn up out of the blue?" Jaela asked.

"I think it would be best," Dr. Pirelli said slowly, "for the Earl to see his daughter before he makes any decision about her."

Jaela looked at Kathy who was sitting on the grass cuddling Betsy, her favourite doll.

She smiled.

"You think he will be captivated by her at first sight?" she asked.

"I am sure of it," the doctor said, "and it would be a mistake to allow him to build up any resentment against her before she even arrives."

Jaela realised that what he was saying was obviously sheer common sense.

For no one could expect the Earl to feel anything but anger at the way that his child had been taken from him when she was so young.

He had apparently heard nothing of her for the last six years.

"You are right," she said having thought it over. "At the same time it is much more complicated than I had expected."

"You are not going to refuse to take her?" Dr. Pirelli asked quickly.

"No, of course not!" Jaela asserted. "I gave the Contessa my word that I would look after Kathy and I will keep it."

*

They set off two days later.

There was only the doctor to wave them goodbye at the Railway Station.

Jaela had arranged for the couple who had been at the Villa since her father and mother had gone there to look after it in their absence.

She assured them that she would definitely be coming back the following spring.

She arranged with her father's Solicitor in Naples that their wages would be paid and that he would inspect the house every month.

She gave the Italian servants a large bonus, which made them profusely grateful.

She also gave them and the doctor her address in London so that they could get in touch with her whenever they wished to do so.

She felt like crying when she finally drove away from the Villa she loved.

She had taken her last look at the fountain, the balcony where she had sat with her father and the rooms that her mother had decorated so exquisitely.

She was saying 'goodbye' to the house which had been her home.

And also to her father and what he had meant to her for the last three years of his life.

Then she remembered that there were two more houses waiting for her that were redolent with his memory.

There was the house in London, where he had lived since his marriage to her mother, and the house in the country.

It was at Mellor Hall that she had spent so much of her time as a child.

'I shall feel that you are beside me, Papa,' she had said before she had left the Villa.

She was reassuring herself that she would not lose him.

*

When the train then started off, Kathy was thrilled with the drawing room car and she told Jaela that it was like a big dolls' house.

She ran from end to end of it and inspected the small pantry where there was food for the journey.

Next she ran into the two bedrooms where she and Jaela were to sleep and then she came back into the drawing room flushed with excitement.

"Betsy thinks this is the best dolls' house she has even been in," she announced.

However, as the train steamed on its way, Kathy became bored with the long journey.

Jaela told her some more stories and read her two or three from the story book that she had been prudent enough to buy before they had left.

Kathy talked incessantly about the pony she would ride and the dog who would play with her.

It all became so real that Jaela was afraid that the Earl would either refuse to give her the animals or else send her away from The Castle.

Then she might have to live with a relative in London or some other town in the North.

Jaela, however, thought wryly that she was frightening herself unnecessarily and it was a mistake to anticipate trouble before one was actually confronted with it.

They slept and ate and then slept again.

It was a relief when they finally reached Paris and at least three-quarters of the journey was now over.

The drawing room car was then attached to the train leaving for Calais.

It was a relief when they could get out of the train to board the Steamer that would carry them to Dover.

The Courier had efficiently arranged for the best cabin on board to be at their disposal.

Kathy, who was longing to move about, ran round the deck.

She was so excited to be on a ship that Jaela was afraid that she might fall overboard.

The doctor had suggested that they might take a maidservant with them, but then Jaela had refused.

"Papa always said that women servants were always tiresome on long journeys and never export well from one country to another."

"I expect that he was right, as he always was," the doctor said, "and so I don't think that Giovanna would want to leave Italy even for a very short time. She is infatuated with one of the men who work in the garden."

Jaela laughed.

"It is always a question of love with the Italians!"

"But of course," Dr. Pirelli replied. "What is more natural?"

Jaela was quite content to look after Kathy herself and, every hour that she was with the child, she loved her more. She was so pretty and at the same time sweet and quick-brained.

She remembered what she had been told and was able to repeat word for word anything that Jaela wanted her to remember.

The English Channel was nicely calm and Jaela exercised herself by walking round the deck with Kathy as soon as they were under way.

When they had reached Dover, there was a reserved carriage waiting for them and the Courier attended to their luggage.

Jaela thought that she had never travelled more comfortably.

She had decided that they would spend the first night in England at the house in London that had belonged to her father and it was odd to think that now it was hers, just as she owned the house in the country and the Villa in Italy.

'I suppose I am rich,' she thought, 'but possessions are not as important as people and I have very few friends.'

She reckoned, however, that their neighbours in the country would indeed welcome her when she returned to Mellor Hall.

There were also a great number of people in London who had been close friends of both her father and her mother, but once again she was up against the barrier that she was in deep mourning.

So she could only attend small intimate functions and would be expected to be draped in black.

She had made no effort before she had left Italy and anyway there had been no time to buy clothes.

She was therefore dressed in the soft flower colours that had always pleased her father.

'I will worry about myself,' she reflected, 'when I can stop worrying about Kathy.'

She had not informed the caretakers in the house in London that she was coming.

They arrived late in the evening.

The old butler when he opened the door to them was astonished to see her.

"Miss Jaela!" he exclaimed. "I must be a-dreamin'."

"No, I am here," Jaela replied, "and I hope now that I am, Dawson, you and your wife will look after me and this little girl for tonight."

~40~

"Of course we will, Miss Jaela," Dawson answered, "and the beds are clean and made up just in case you and the Master ever turned up unexpected like."

Jaela drew in her breath.

Before she could say anything, however, Dawson went on,

"We were that upset, Miss Jaela, when we hears about how the Master had died. Mrs. Dawson, she wept her eyes out, she did."

"He – did not suffer," Jaela managed to say, making an effort to control her tears.

Then the luggage that was outside in the carriage with the Courier had to be taken into the house.

*

Later, having listened to a weeping Mrs. Dawson saying how much they had both loved her father and that things would never be the same without him, Jaela felt that she could bear no more.

She knew if she notified any of her relatives that she was in London, she would have to talk and go on talking about her father's last days.

There would be endless details that they would want to know about both her father's and her mother's deaths.

'I just cannot bear it,' Jaela told herself when she was alone.

The agony of loss was bad enough without feeling as if every word that she had to say was turning a knife in an open wound.

She knew without her saying so that Mrs. Dawson was somewhat surprised that she was not in black and she knew that her relatives would be really horrified.

Before she saw any of them she would have to go shopping.

Then she remembered that the first thing she had to do was to take Kathy to her father.

And after that she could begin to think of herself.

Lying on her own bed with Kathy sleeping peacefully next door, Jaela made a decision.

She would try to persuade the Earl to let her stay at The Castle for a few days, perhaps a week.

It would be not only for Kathy's sake but also for her own.

She well knew that she could never be happy unless she was quite certain that Kathy had fitted into her new environment.

'She might easily feel very lonely and lost, which is how I am at the moment,' Jaela told herself, 'and it is a really miserable feeling.'

Her last resolution before she fell fast asleep was that she must persuade the Earl that her presence was so essential to Kathy's happiness and she was optimistic enough to think that he would understand.

*

The following morning when she came downstairs she found that there was a telegraph for her.

As it was from Italy, she guessed, even before she opened it, what it contained.

"Contessa died peacefully this morning.
PIRELLI."

She read it twice and then tore it up.

She knew that it would be a mistake to tell Kathy that her mother was dead while they were travelling.

It would be wiser to wait until the right moment when the child had other things to think about.

Because Kathy was tired and slept very late, they spent two nights in London.

The Courier had made all the arrangements for them to travel to Lincolnshire where Hale Castle was situated.

Then he said 'goodbye' and Jaela rewarded him handsomely for his excellent services.

She had packed up a silver cigarette case that had belonged to her father for him to give to Dr. Pirelli. It was inscribed with his initials and she hoped that he would appreciate it.

She also wrote a letter to him to say how grateful she was for all his help and kindness.

Finally she instructed Dawson that on no account was he to inform any of her friends or relations that she was in England.

Then Jaela left the London house with Kathy and their luggage for a train that would carry them to Lincolnshire.

The Courier had found out that there was a Private Halt where the train would stop for any guests travelling to Hale Castle.

Kathy was very excited by this.

"My Papa has a little Station all to himself!" she exclaimed.

The child kept looking out of the window and asked at every Station they stopped at if it was her father's.

Finally the train came to a standstill where a signpost told them that it was the Halt for Hale Castle.

Kathy was entranced.

Unfortunately the very old porter who worked on the signals informed them that there was no conveyance to carry them to Hale Castle.

It was the one thing, Jaela thought, that she had overlooked and so had the Courier.

She had imagined that there would be a carriage of some sort at the Private Halt.

She was dismayed when she learnt that the distance between the Halt and The Castle was over five miles.

The train moved away and she stood on the platform looking helplessly at the porter.

"What do you suggest we do?" she asked him.

He shook his head.

"I don't knows, miss."

"There must be a vehicle of some sort that we could hire?" Jaela asked hopefully.

Finally, after she had questioned him for a long time, she discovered one.

A farmer would be coming late in the afternoon with produce to be put on the morning train to the nearest town.

"Where can we go until then?" Jaela asked.

She told herself that she had been stupid not to have realised that this part of England was sparsely populated and, standing on the small platform of the Halt, there appeared to be nothing but green fields and trees stretching to an indefinite horizon.

After a while the porter took them to his cottage where he said that his 'Missus' would make them a nice cup of tea.

At least it would be better than waiting in the platform shelter, Jaela thought, which had only two hard wooden benches inside it.

She accepted the porter's offer gratefully and he led her and Kathy down a steep incline and tucked away amongst some low trees was his cottage.

It was very small and occupied only by the porter and his wife.

She was a large cheerful woman who obviously found their situation lonely.

So she was now delighted to have someone to talk to.

She produced a glass of warm milk for Kathy and poured out a cup of very strong tea for Jaela.

While she did so, she never stopped talking.

She was also extremely curious as to why they were going to visit Hale Castle.

It was Kathy who told her the truth.

"I am going to see my Papa," she piped up, "and he is going to give me a pony to ride and a dog of my very own."

"Your Papa?" the porter's wife exclaimed with astonishment. "Then you're little Lady Katherine. I've often wondered what 'ad 'appened to you."

After that the words gushed out of her like a tidal wave.

She had wondered, as everybody in the neighbourhood had wondered, what had become of the Countess.

"'Tis not surprisin', seein' 'ow pretty her were, and Lady Katherine's grown into a very pretty little girl."

On and on she talked until Jaela began to feel dizzy at the flow of her words.

One blessing was she did not have to say anything, she only had to listen.

She learned how no one could imagine after the Countess went away what had happened to her and why she never came back.

The Earl had announced that she was ill and had been sent to a warmer climate.

First one year, then two years passed, before everybody rightly assumed that she would never return.

"Then some very strange things 'appened," the porter's wife said lowering her voice.

Jaela guessed what was coming and looked quickly at Kathy.

The child was curled up in an armchair in front of the fire and she was nursing her doll and was talking to it in a low voice.

Jaela felt that she should not be listening to all the gossip of the porter's wife, but despite herself she was curious.

"Ever such a pretty lady comes to The Castle," she was saying, "a real lady, she was! Me 'usband 'ears that even the Prince of Wales 'ad fancied 'er when she were in London."

"What was her name?" Jaela asked curiously.

She realised that it was a mistake to gossip, but at the same time she just could not help wanting to know more than what she had heard already.

The porter's wife frowned.

"There now," she said, "t'were 'Lady – somethin', but now it's slipped me mind for the moment and what d'you think 'appened?"

She went on to relate that the lady had stayed very often at The Castle and she had been seen out riding with the Earl on a number of occasions.

And everybody expected that sooner or later he would marry her.

"Then 'e'd be wantin' a divorce," the porter's wife said, "and, seein' as the Countess'd been away for so long, they said as there'd be no difficulty 'bout it."

Jaela knew, however, what had happened.

"Then she disappeared," the porter's wife related in a voice hardly above a whisper. "Me niece as works up at The Castle and be one of the 'ousemaids, she says as how one day 'er were there the next 'er weren't."

Jaela was listening intently, it was impossible not to.

"She jest vanished!" the porter's wife carried on with relish. "All 'er clothes was in 'er bedroom, 'er jewels and everythin' else she possessed."

"How could she just have disappeered like that?" Jaela asked.

"There be no answer to that," the porter's wife replied. "They searches the grounds, the woods, they drags the lake, but there be neither sight nor sound of 'er!"

"It certainly seems extraordinary!" Jaela agreed.

There was nothing else the porter's wife could say and no further details.

She merely repeated herself over and over again.

It was therefore a relief when just after six o'clock the porter, who had been up to the Halt two or three times, came back.

The farmer was there with his gig.

"'E'll take you to The Castle, miss," he said to Jaela, "but it's a lot out of 'is way."

Jaela knew from the way the man spoke that she was expected to pay rather heavily for the ride.

She said quickly,

"I am, of course, very very grateful and I will reward him for his trouble."

The porter smiled and came back a little later to say that their luggage was in the gig and the farmer wanted to leave at once.

Jaela thanked the porter's wife profusely.

She tactfully enquired if she would buy herself a little memento of the happy hours that they had spent in her cottage.

She at first refused then, as Jaela insisted and quickly slipped the golden guineas into the pocket of her apron.

Kathy was at first thrilled at the idea of sitting on the hard seat between the farmer and Jaela. He was driving behind a young horse that fortunately moved swiftly.

But by the time The Castle was in sight, the child was almost asleep.

Jaela knew that she would have had to stifle a yawn if she had not been apprehensive at arriving so late.

The farmer himself was a taciturn old man who had no wish to talk as he concentrated on his driving and it was a relief to be silent after having been obliged to listen for so long to the porter's wife.

When they drove down the long drive of oak trees, she was glad to see the lights shining golden in the windows of the huge building.

Hale Castle was impressive and, although it was nearly dark, Jaela could see the Earl's standard flying on top of the highest Tower.

They drew up outside the great front door with a number of stone steps leading up to it.

As the gig came to a standstill, the door opened and a footman in a smart Livery looked out in surprise.

Jaela stepped down without anyone helping her and then lifted Kathy to the ground.

She had three sovereigns ready in her hand which she gave to the farmer, thanking him profusely for his kindness.

By this time the footman had reached the bottom of the steps and then before Jaela could speak the farmer said,

"You'll 'ave to get the luggage out the back, boy. Me 'orse'll move off if I let 'im!"

The footman looked surprised.

"Perhaps you ought to ask somebody to help you," Jaela suggested. "There are quite a number of trunks."

As she spoke, she saw another footman and the butler come to the top of the steps.

Taking Kathy by the hand, she walked up them.

"Good evening, ma'am" the butler said with an obvious question in his voice.

"Is the Earl of Halesworth at home?" Jaela asked.

It had not struck her until she asked the question that the Earl might be away, in which case she might be in a very difficult position.

"His Lordship is in residence, ma'am," the butler replied, "but he didn't inform me that he was expectin' visitors."

"Will you please tell his Lordship," Jaela said, "that I need to see him on a matter of the greatest importance?"

As she spoke, she walked through the front door and into the hall.

Then, as she saw the butler staring at Kathy in puzzlement, she announced,

"This is Lady Katherine Worth!"

The butler drew in a deep breath.

"She's very like her Ladyship," he said as if he spoke to himself.

Then remembering his duties he added,

"Will you please come this way, ma'am?"

He led Jaela and Kathy across the hall.

Then opening a door he showed them into a room where there was a large fire burning brightly.

Jaela took Kathy towards it and she had known that she had felt cold perched up in the farmer's gig although Jaela had put her arms around her.

Now she lifted Kathy into an armchair, which she pushed a little nearer to the fire.

Then she realised that the butler was still standing in the room behind her.

As she looked at him, she saw an expression of indecision on his face and then she said quietly,

"Please inform his Lordship that we are here – but perhaps it would be best to leave it to me to tell him that I have his daughter with me."

"Much, much the best, ma'am," the butler replied hastily.

He walked towards the door and, as he reached it, he said,

"I'll tell his Lordship, as you says at first, that you've called on a matter of importance."

He did not wait for a reply, but closed the door behind him.

When he had gone, Jaela had the uncomfortable feeling that he was most definitely too frightened to tell the Earl the truth.

CHAPTER THREE

Jaela sat down by the fire.

She realised that Kathy was silent and obviously very tired.

She was holding her doll closely to her chest and watching the flames springing up over the logs.

Jaela felt as if she was in a theatre and the curtain was going to rise and she was not at all certain what she would see.

She was now becoming frightened.

After this long journey, when they were both very tired, the Earl might be difficult.

The door opened and she looked round apprehensively, but it was the butler who then came into the room.

He walked towards her and, when he was by her side said,

"His Lordship's dressin' for dinner but I've given him your message and he says he'll be down later."

He paused before he added,

"His Lordship did suggest that you could come back tomorrow, but I tells him that was impossible."

"Thank you," Jaela said with a smile.

"As there's a bit of time to wait, is there anythin' I can get her Ladyship and you?"

"We were looked after by the porter's wife at the Halt," Jaela replied.

The butler gave an exclamation.

"I wonders why you came here in Farmer Fielding's gig."

"There was no other conveyance," Jaela told him, "and it was foolish of me not to expect that."

The butler nodded.

He put two more logs on the fire and left the room.

Jaela waited and a little later she realised that Kathy was fast asleep on the sofa.

She removed the child's bonnet and her fair hair against the silk cushion looked lovely.

She thought that any man who was not pleased with such a pretty daughter would have a heart of stone.

Time passed.

She kept glancing at the clock on the mantelpiece and thinking that every minute seemed like an hour.

Suddenly the door opened.

And, as she rose to her feet, the Earl came into the room.

She had expected him to be overpowering but in his evening clothes he was magnificent.

She had also not expected him to look so young or so handsome.

Yet, as he drew nearer to her, she was aware there were cynical lines running from his nose to his mouth.

There was nothing genial in the expression in his eyes as he looked at her.

"You wanted to see me?" he asked in a lofty and what she thought was a rather arrogant tone. "I was informed that it was a matter of urgency."

Jaela dropped him a small curtsey.

"I have, my Lord," she said slowly, "brought your daughter home to you."

As she spoke, she indicated Kathy with her hand.

When the Earl turned his head, he could then see the child.

He stiffened.

Although he did not speak, she could feel the anger emanating from him.

Then he asked harshly,

"On whose authority has this child been sent here"

"I have brought her to you, my Lord, from Italy."

"Then you can take her straight back again!" the Earl said sharply. "And you can inform her mother that it is too late for me to acknowledge her as my daughter."

He turned as he spoke as if to walk away.

Next Jaela said quickly

"I am afraid, my Lord, that is impossible."

"Why?"

"Because the Countess is dead!"

Again the Earl was still before he repeated beneath his breath,

"Dead?"

It was obviously something that he had not anticipated.

Jaela was silent.

After what seemed a long time, the Earl asked her,

"How did she die"

"Both her lungs were infected," Jaela explained, "and there was no way of saving her."

The Earl moved to the sofa where Kathy was sleeping.

He looked down at her and then he said in the same abrupt tone that he had used before,

"What happened to the man she was with?"

"I understand the Conte, my Lord, has returned to his own wife and family."

Jaela saw the Earl's lips tighten in a hard line and he turned to look at her saying in what she thought was a contemptuous voice,

"And where do you figure in this abominable situation?"

Almost as if she was being prompted, Jaela knew what she must answer.

If she said that she was a friend, he would obviously send her away.

She would be unable to look after Kathy, as she had promised the Contessa she would and, in a voice that hardly seemed like her own, she replied,

"I-I am Kathy's – Governess!"

"And you brought the child here at her mother's request?"

"It was her doctor who asked me to take Kathy away because he was afraid of her being infected by the disease. But it was in fact only a question of days before the – Countess died."

She stumbled over the title, having nearly said 'Contessa' and she thought that the Earl was aware of it.

"You are her Governess," he said reflecting after a moment's pause. "Are you prepared to stay here with her?"

"It is what I would like to do, my Lord," Jaela replied. "Kathy has lived a very lonely life in Italy and, of course, everything in England will seem very strange to her."

Then the Earl obviously made up his mind.

"Very well," he replied, "You will stay here in The Castle and I will speak to you about it further in the morning."

After another look at Kathy, he walked away down the room.

As he left the door ajar, Jaela could hear his voice giving orders in the hall.

She waited and about five minutes later an elderly woman in rustling black silk with a silver chatelaine at her waist came hurrying into the room.

"How d'you do then, miss," she said to Jaela. "When they tells me you'd brought Lady Katherine back home, you could have knocked me down with a feather!"

As she shook Jaela's hand, she turned towards the sofa.

Looking at Kathy she then said,

"The living image of her mother! I'd have known her anywhere. And the poor child's tired out, that's for sure!"

"We have come – a long way," Jaela told her quietly.

She had already decided that it would be a mistake to say that they had stayed in London.

She might be questioned as to where they had stayed and with whom.

Having said that she was the Governess, she need not change her name, she determined.

Kathy had already called her 'Miss Compton' and it was a common name in England and there was no reason therefore why anybody should connect it with her famous father.

The housekeeper called one of the footmen to carry Kathy upstairs.

As he lifted her up, she gave a little murmur and she opened her eyes then closed them again, obviously to return to her dreams.

The housekeeper went first and the footman carrying Kathy followed her.

Jaela, holding Kathy's bonnet, came behind.

When they reached the top of the stairs, the housekeeper related,

"The nurseries are just as they were when her Ladyship left us. You may think it strange that they're on the first floor, but her mother, God rest her soul, wanted her baby to be near to her."

She turned left and now Jaela guessed that the State rooms would be on the right.

They went a little way down the corridor and the housekeeper then opened a door.

A maid was lighting the gas lamps in one of the prettiest nurseries that Jaela had ever seen.

She was not in the least surprised, seeing how lovely the Villa in Italy had been.

The white rooms with their fine pictures must she thought have reflected the Countess's taste as well as the Conte's.

Now in the nurseries that Kathy had used as a baby, Jaela saw that the walls were a very pale pink.

The curtains were bright with flowers and there was a screen covered with Christmas and Valentine cards, which she was sure that the Countess must have made herself.

The footman crossed the nursery to the night nursery that opened out of it and, as Jaela followed him, she saw that this room too was very pretty.

There was a draped cot in one corner, which was now too small for Kathy.

There was, however, a single bed that must have been used by her Nanny.

The footman put the child very gently down on it.

She did not stir but went on sleeping.

"Thank you, James," the housekeeper said, "and now see that the luggage is brought up as quickly as possible."

"Right away, Mrs. Hudson," the footman replied.

"I'll show you where you'll be sleepin'," the housekeeper said to Jaela, "and now I come to think of it, you've not yet told me your name."

"It is Compton – Jaela Compton."

"Well, I think you'll be comfortable, Miss Compton, but if you do want anythin', you just have to ask me."

"Thank you," Jaela said.

"I expect now you'll be wantin' somethin' to eat," Mrs. Hudson said, "and I'll tell chef to prepare you a nice meal, although I expects her Ladyship'll be too tired to want anythin' tonight."

"I am sure she will," Jaela replied. "It has been a very long journey for a very small girl."

"I can hardly believe you're here," Mrs. Hudson exclaimed. "We've all been wonderin' what had happened to her Ladyship and little Lady Katherine."

"She calls herself 'Kathy'," Jaela pointed out.

"That's pretty," Mrs. Hudson smiled. "And if she does grow up like her mother, she'll be pretty as a picture, that's what she'll be."

"She is already," Jaela replied.

While they were talking, two footmen were bringing in the luggage and they put it all in Jaela's bedroom.

But it took up too much room and Mrs. Hudson ordered some of it to be left outside on the landing.

"Elsie'll unpack what you'll need for tonight," she said.

It was sometime before her nightgown and the other things that Jaela may require were found.

In the meantime she undressed Kathy who was too sleepy to know what was happening to her.

Elsie the maid was willing to help her, but Jaela wanted to look after the child herself.

Two hours later she had a last look at Kathy before she too went to bed.

She thought that on the whole things had gone better than she might have expected.

At least they had not been sent away immediately.

This was what the Earl had intended when he was first told who Kathy was.

Now that he had accepted the child, he would be charmed by her as everybody else was.

All the same, when she was in bed, Jaela sent up a very special prayer to the Contessa, wherever she might be.

'I am trying to help Kathy,' she said, 'but please persuade her father to let me stay here at least for a little while with her. I could not bear her to be unhappy or frightened.'

As she finished praying, she thought that she herself found the Earl very frightening.

When she was waiting for him to make up his mind, she had held her breath.

When he had then walked away without looking back, her heart had been thumping in her breast.

'It will all seem much better in the morning,' she mused optimistically before falling into a deep sleep.

*

Kathy was awake at seven o'clock.

Jaela had left the doors open in case she woke up in the night and became frightened in a strange place.

Now she came running into her bedroom in her nightgown.

"We are in The Castle, Miss Compton," she enthused, "and it is so very exciting to be here!"

"That is what I thought," Jaela said, "and, of course, we must explore it all and see what we can find."

"Let's do that at once," Kathy exclaimed.

"I think we had better get dressed first and, of course, you want some breakfast," Jaela smiled.

"I am hungry, very hungry," Kathy asserted, "and I missed my supper last night."

"You did," Jaela said. "But you will be able to make up for it today."

She rang the bell and Elsie came into the nursery at once.

Elsie dressed Kathy while Jaela dressed herself.

By the time they were ready, breakfast was being brought upstairs.

It was a real English breakfast.

There was porridge to start with, which Kathy had never eaten before.

Then there were eggs and bacon, a cottage loaf fresh from the oven, toast, marmalade and honey.

Kathy did not like the porridge, but Jaela added brown sugar and cream in the middle of it and she remembered that it was what her Nanny had always done for her.

Kathy then ate all the porridge and found the eggs and bacon delicious. She also had a large slice of new bread spread with butter and comb honey.

"Now I feel better, Miss Compton," she said. "Let's go and explore The Castle."

"I think first," Jaela replied, "you should meet your father."

"I am going to ask Papa for my pony," Kathy insisted firmly.

Jaela did not say anything.

She merely took Kathy by the hand and they went down the stairs.

There was a footman on duty in the hall and she asked him,

"Where can I find his Lordship?"

"'E be in the breakfast room, miss," the footman replied.

The butler then appeared, whose name Jaela learned from Elsie was 'Whitlock'.

"Are you wantin' to see his Lordship, Miss Compton?" Whitlock asked.

"I thought her Ladyship should meet her father," Jaela said in a low voice.

He nodded.

She knew that he understood that this was an important moment.

He took them down the corridor and opened a door.

Without him saying anything, Jaela knew he was thinking that Kathy should go in alone.

There was a screen in front of the door to keep out the draughts and Jaela pushed Kathy forward.

In her white dress with the blue sash she looked like a child out of a Fairy Story.

No man, she thought, could ask for a lovelier daughter.

Having been brought up in Italy, Kathy had never been shy and she walked into the room where the Earl was sitting at the top of the table.

The morning newspaper was propped up on a silver stand in front of him.

She had only taken a very few steps towards him when from under the table emerged three spaniels.

Two of them wagged their tails, while the third gave a warning growl.

"Be careful!" the Earl commanded sharply but it was too late.

Kathy had seen the dogs and gave a cry of delight.

"Dogs!" she cried. "*Dogs*! And I want one of my very own."

She went down on her knees.

She put her arms round two of the spaniels, who wagged their tails frantically and licked her face.

The third spaniel, as if not to be left out, came nearer and she patted it saying,

"You are lovely. The most beautiful dogs I have ever seen. Oh, please, Papa, may I have one of my very own?"

The Earl, who had been watching her in some surprise said after a moment,

"I think first you should say 'good morning' to me."

Kathy laughed.

"The dogs said 'good morning' to me first, Papa, and I did not have time to curtsey as Miss Compton said I should."

She then made him a little curtsey and put up her face to be kissed.

For a moment the Earl hesitated.

Then, because Kathy was waiting, his lips just brushed her skin.

"Now I have said 'good morning'," Kathy said, "can I please, Papa, have a pony all of my own?"

"It that what you expect me to give you?" the Earl asked her.

"Miss Compton said you would have lots and lots of horses and she was sure that there would be room in your stables for a pony."

"And you apparently also want a dog."

Kathy gave a deep sigh.

"I have longed and longed for a dog, but Mama said Uncle Diego said it would be a nuisance in the Villa."

Listening to this conversation Jaela held her breath.

She had not thought to tell the child not to mention the Conte and she wondered now what would happen.

"You shall have a dog," the Earl said, "and perhaps, as they are already house-trained, you should at first have one of mine."

"One of these you have here?" Kathy said. "Oh, Papa, that would be lovely. And I will explain that it belongs to me and must sleep at the bottom of my bed."

"Which one do you want?" the Earl asked.

Kathy knelt down on the floor and once again was caressing the dogs.

They were only too willing to be patted and hugged and finally she chose one that was a little smaller than the other two.

It was a well-bred and very good-looking spaniel.

"Please, Papa, may I have this one?" she asked the Earl.

"That is Rufus," the Earl replied, "because his coat is so red."

Kathy put her arms around the dog and hugged him.

"I love you, Rufus," she sighed, "and now you are mine, my very own."

Then she jumped up from the floor and almost shouted,

"Thank you, *thank you,* Papa! You are very kind and I want to kiss you."

The Earl inclined his head, but Kathy put her arms around his neck.

When she released him, the Earl, as if he was slightly embarrassed, asked her,

"What do you want to do now?"

Kathy put her head on one side.

"Perhaps it would be greedy when you have given me one present to ask for another," she replied, "but I do so want a pony of my own too."

The Earl laughed.

"I see it is only a question of time before you have an insatiable desire for jewels!"

Kathy did not understand, but she suggested,

"If we are going to go and look at my pony, shall I tell Miss Compton I want my coat and my bonnet?"

"You may want a coat," the Earl answered, "but there is no need for you to be dressed up when you are in the country. And you had better tell your Governess to come too. I am not having you taking any risks with the horses when I am not there."

"I will tell her, *I will tell her!*" Kathy cried excitedly and ran from the room.

Jaela just had time to slip from behind the screen and out into the corridor.

Kathy then flung herself against her.

"I want my coat, Miss Compton," she said, "and Papa says you are to come and look at the pony, my pony, the pony I am to have all of my own."

"We will get your coat," Jaela smiled.

As she spoke, Whitlock told a footman to run upstairs and collect their coats from Elsie.

It was only a question of a few minutes before he came back with them.

Jaela had taken Kathy to the bottom of the stairs and, as she buttoned her into a pretty blue coat trimmed with white braid, the Earl came into the hall and said,

"Good morning, Miss Compton."

Jaela curtseyed.

"Good morning, my Lord."

"I understand from my daughter that she wishes to have a pony and it was your idea."

He spoke accusingly and Jaela replied,

"She has been thinking of little else, my Lord, since we set out for England."

"Has the child ridden before?"

"Yes, I believe she has."

"Then you have not been with her for long?"

"No, my Lord."

The Earl had been followed into the hall by his three dogs and he was aware that, while he had been talking, Kathy had been patting Rufus and making a considerable fuss of him.

Now calling his name she ran out through the front door and down the steps.

The Earl and Jaela followed her.

With the dog at her heels Kathy ran across the courtyard, then stopped and hugged him.

She looked very lovely with the sun glinting on her very fair hair.

Jaela could not help glancing up at the Earl to see what he was thinking.

To her surprise, he said to her in what she thought was an unnecessarily hard voice,

"I am now taking you to the stables, Miss Compton, so that you will make quite sure that Katherine does not behave with the horses in just the same way that she is behaving with my dogs. She is obviously not afraid of animals, but it is a mistake to take any risks with them."

"I understand that, my Lord," Jaela said, "but then, of course, Kathy is English and the English have a way with animals that foreigners do not understand."

"What do you mean they have 'a way with animals'?" the Earl asked.

There was a sarcastic note in his voice.

"I suppose it is because they love them," Jaela replied. "Most Englishmen ride well and have obedient dogs, which is something that you don't often find in other European countries with the exception of Hungary."

She was talking in the same way as she might have spoken to her father.

The Earl looked at her in surprise.

Only then did she think that it was perhaps not what an ordinary Governess might have said.

"Am I to understand from the way that you are talking, that you ride yourself?" the Earl enquired.

Jaela laughed.

"I have ridden, my Lord, since I was three and I am hoping that you will allow me to take Kathy on a leading rein."

She thought as she spoke that she had been somewhat presumptuous and the Earl might easily say that he would prefer one of his grooms to do so.

He merely made no answer, but walked towards the stables.

Kathy, seeing the direction that they were going in, followed behind them.

They passed under a stone archway that lay some distance from the house and then she ran to her father to slip her hand into his.

"Have you really a pony in your stables, Papa?" she asked him. "Miss Compton said at breakfast that I was not to be disappointed if you only had horses that were too big for me."

"As it happens, I have a pony," the Earl replied. "I bought it two years ago for a cousin of yours, a boy called 'Ian', who came to stay with his parents for Christmas."

"But you did not let Ian take it away with him?" Kathy wanted to know anxiously.

"If I had, you would be very disappointed, because there would be no pony for you here now."

Kathy considered this and then she said,

"I am glad, very glad, Papa, that you kept the pony."

The Earl was now greeting the Head Groom.

"Good morning, Pearson."

"A fine marnin', my Lord, and I've got Thunderer ready for you."

"Before I take him for a ride," the Earl said, "I want to see the pony we bought two years ago. Lady Katherine wishes to ride him."

Pearson touched his forelock.

"Good marnin', your Ladyship," he said to Kathy. "It be good to 'ave you back with us."

"If you have a pony for me, I want to ride him at once," Kathy said.

"It'll be a very good thing if you do just that, my Lady," Pearson answered. "Snowball be gettin' fat through lack of exercise."

"Is his name really 'Snowball'?" Kathy asked delightedly.

"It be and I'll 'ave 'e brought out right away for you."

Pearson called a stable lad who ran down the yard.

"Come and look at my horses," the Earl suggested.

They went through the first stable door and Jaela followed.

She had expected the Earl's horses to be truly magnificent. But when she looked in first one stall and then another she knew that they were outstanding.

They were just the sort of horses that her father had ridden when they were in the country but there were many more of them.

Also she had to admit the stallions were finer than any that she had ever seen.

She forgot about the Earl and Kathy as she moved from one stall to another.

She knew that, if she had to describe them, she would run out of adjectives.

Then she heard Kathy give a cry of excitement and ran out into the yard and she realised that the pony must have been brought out for her inspection.

She hurried after her and, as she reached the child, the Earl said sharply,

"You appear to have already forgotten what I have said to you, Miss Compton. The way Katherine is behaving would make it likely for any horse to lash out at her."

"I am sorry, my Lord," Jaela said, "I was so bemused by your fine horses."

The Earl did not seem to be appeased by her explanation as he was frowning as he lifted Kathy up onto the saddle of the pony.

It was aptly called 'Snowball' because he was white.

Kathy picked up the reins in quite an experienced manner and pleaded beguilingly,

"Please, Papa, may I take Snowball for a ride?"

"You are not dressed for riding," the Earl reminded her, "but the groom could lead you a little way down the drive."

"I want to ride very very fast!" Kathy stated.

"Not until I am quite certain that you can ride well," the Earl said firmly.

Kathy indicated to the young groom who had been holding the pony's head that she was ready.

They started and rode out of the yard.

"I am riding! *I am riding!*" Kathy cried excitedly.

"Go with the child," the Earl said to Jaela, "and today she is only to be led. Tomorrow, when she is dressed properly and if I consider her to be safe, I will allow you to take her on a leading rein."

"Thank you, my Lord," Jaela exclaimed.

But the Earl had already turned away.

He was mounting Thunderer, which had now been brought into the yard for him and the three spaniels were waiting to go with him.

But at that moment Kathy looked back and saw them.

"Rufus! *Rufus!*" she called out.

The spaniel hesitated and then, as Kathy called him again, the dog obeyed her.

He turned to follow her out from the yard and Jaela did the same.

As she walked on down the drive, she thought that the child had taken her first fences in style.

If everything continued as well as it was doing at the moment, she would soon be free to think about herself and her future.

At the same time she knew that she wanted to ride the same sort of horses that the Earl was riding.

She thought that, when she went back to Mellor Hall, she would definitely spend quite a lot of her money on filling the stables with fine thoroughbreds.

They had been emptied when her father and mother had moved to Italy and she thought with satisfaction that they were very good stables.

It would be a delight to have superb horses in them.

When the autumn came she would be able to ride and join the local Hunt of which her father had been a member and she was sure that there would be a number of young people of her own age in the neighbourhood.

Then she looked ahead and saw Kathy laughing and talking excitedly to the stable boy.

She knew then with unmistakable certainty that she had no wish to leave the child at the moment.

It seemed ridiculous when she had known her for such a short time.

Yet she loved Kathy and there was no doubt that Kathy loved her.

Later, when Kathy's pony had been returned to the stables, Jaela looked into the garden.

"Will you ride with me tomorrow, Miss Compton?" Kathy said. "I would like that and I will not have to be on a leading-rein all the time, will I?"

"You heard what your father said," Jaela replied. "You will have to ride very very well before he lets you ride without one."

"I ride well now," Kathy objected. "Uncle Diego said so."

"I think, Kathy," Jaela said quietly, "it would be a mistake for you to talk about Uncle Diego now that you are at The Castle."

"Why?" Kathy asked.

Jaela hesitated and then she thought that it was best to be frank.

"Your Papa does not like him."

Kathy was silent and then she asked,

"Why does Papa not like Uncle Diego?"

They were walking over the lawn and Jaela stopped at a wooden seat.

"Let us sit down, Kathy," she said. "I want to talk to you for a moment."

Kathy climbed onto the seat beside her and she said,

"I want you to promise me not to talk about Uncle Diego and not to say very much about Italy."

"Does Papa not like Italy?" Kathy enquired.

"You father was sad because you went away with your Mama and lived in Italy and left him alone. Now you are here with him you just want to remember that you are English and The Castle is your home and forget about the Villa and all the things that happened there with your mother."

"I love Mama," Kathy emphasised.

"Of course you do and you will always remember her in your prayers."

"When Mama is well, I will go back to Italy and be with her?" Kathy persisted.

Jaela debated whether she should tell her the truth. Then, because she was afraid that she might learn it from the servants, she said,

"Now I want you to be very brave, Kathy, when I tell you that your mother is very happy because she is in Heaven."

"Is she with the angels?" Kathy asked.

"With the angels and she is thinking of you all the time and loving you and she wants you to be happy here with your Papa."

"If Mama is – with the angels," Kathy said slowly, "then – she is – dead!"

"Yes, Kathy," Jaela said softly, "but you must think of her in Heaven, well and happy with no pain and surrounded by all the beautiful things, like the flowers, the sunshine and the music that she loved on earth."

There was silence while Kathy thought this over and then she said,

"I want Mama! I want to be with her, even if I cannot – touch her,"

"What you have to remember," Jaela said, "is that your Mama is with you, even though you cannot see her. At night, when you are in bed, if you think about her, she will be there, looking after you and she will tell you what to do so that you will be happy and kind to other people."

"Will she really be here with me – in The Castle?" Kathy asked.

"Yes, she will," Jaela said.

"Then I will talk to her – tonight."

"And I am sure you will find that she answers you," Jaela said, "only it is something you hear with your heart and not with your ears."

"That sounds funny," Kathy almost smiled.

Rufus put his paws up on the seat beside her and she asked,

"Can I run across the lawn with Rufus?"

"Yes, of course, you can and see who can run the fastest, you or him."

Kathy climbed down and, calling to the dog she ran as fast as her small legs could carry her.

She went over the green lawn and into a Bowling Green that led out beyond it.

Jaela gave a deep sigh, she had been afraid of telling Kathy that her mother was dead.

It had actually been easier than she had expected.

She had been so afraid that the child would be desperately unhappy.

It was the best thing that could happen that she had so much that was new and exciting to absorb her in at the moment.

There would not be that aching emptiness that she herself felt when she thought of her father.

She was sure that he would be amused at the idea of her pretending to be a Governess when she had a fortune of her own. Also two houses at her disposal, not to mention the Villa in Italy.

'As soon as Kathy is really happy here,' she thought, 'I will go back to London.'

Then she remembered the tears that Mrs. Dawson had shed.

She shrank from encountering the grief of her relatives.

'They will never believe, as I do, Papa, that you are alive and near me,' she said as she walked after Kathy, 'but I know that you are there, guiding me and I know that it was you who thought I should pretend to be a Governess.'

She could hear her father laughing and she went on,

'I am quite sure that the Earl will cross-examine me as to what I am teaching Kathy and he is certain to say that it is all wrong!'

She smiled to herself as she continued,

'What do you think of him, Papa? I can understand the Contessa finding him so difficult and perhaps he was continually finding fault with her as he does with me.'

She laughed aloud as she added,

'Of course I can give in my 'notice' and there will be nothing he can do about it!'

Then she saw Kathy running back towards her.

She knew that for a little while she had no wish to leave The Castle.

Kathy reached her and flung her arms around her waist.

"I can run as fast as Rufus, Miss Compton," she boasted. "I can! *I can*! And he is panting because he ran so quickly."

CHAPTER FOUR

Jaela had just finished an excellent dinner.

She was sitting reading by the fire in the nursery when Mrs. Hudson came into the room.

"I come to see if you've everythin' you want, Miss Compton."

"Everything, thank you," Jaela replied. "You have been very kind."

Mrs. Hudson sat down in the armchair opposite her.

"Well, it's a real pleasure to have someone young about the place. It's cheered us all up no end."

"I am glad about that," Jaela replied.

"Of course, his Lordship's friends come to stay," Mrs. Hudson said, "but ever since the tragedy they're usually ladies without their husbands."

Jaela looked surprised and Mrs. Hudson exclaimed,

"But what can you really expect with a gentleman who's so good-lookin' besides bein' a sportsman and wealthy."

There was a little pause.

Then Jaela asked her,

"Are you saying that his Lordship is attractive to women?"

"Of course he is!" Mrs. Hudson said. "How could he be anything else? A terrible shock 'twas when her Ladyship goes off after they've only been married for such a very short time. Naturally we realised, though he never says anythin', that she was with that Italian fellow!"

She said the last word in a scathing manner that made Jaela want to laugh.

It was so English, she thought, to suspect foreigners and talk as if they were somehow unnatural.

A little hesitatingly she next said,

"The porter's wife told me about the tragedy."

"That woman'd talk the hind leg off a donkey!" Mrs. Hudson exclaimed. "But 'twere a tragedy and you can't stop people talkin'."

"That is true," Jaela replied, "But what really happened?"

She knew at once that it was a mistake to ask such a question. At the same time it was impossible not to be curious after what Dr. Pirelli had said and then the porter's wife.

Mrs. Hudson settled herself more comfortably in the armchair.

She was obviously only too pleased to be a source of information.

"Lady Anstey," she began, "was a real beauty, there's no doubt about that at all and after she'd finished mournin' for her husband, who was a soldier and was killed in the East, she was the talk of London."

Jaela noted the name, which she had now heard for the first time.

"Her picture were in the magazines," Mrs. Hudson went on, "and it didn't surprise us, after she'd stayed here two or three times, that 'twas obvious his Lordship found her ever so attractive."

"How old was she?" Jaela asked.

"Oh, about twenty-five, I would suppose," Mrs. Hudson replied, "and at the height of her beauty."

She paused for a few moments before she added,

"I'll find a picture of her and show you, but we soon knows what she were aimin' at."

"What was that?" Jaela enquired.

"She wanted to marry his Lordship, and 'twas not surprisin', seein' how handsome he is, and also Lady Anstey were not well off."

"And did he want to marry her?" Jaela enquired.

Mrs. Hudson lowered her voice, although there was no one in the nursery to overhear her.

"Just by chance I were passin' the boudoir adjoinin' her Ladyship's bedroom and I hears his Lordship say – "

Her voice dropped even lower.

Jaela's eyes twinkled because she reckoned that Mrs. Hudson had been eavesdropping.

"'It is no use, Myrtle,' he says, 'I am a married man and it is impossible for me to marry anyone!'

"'Don't be so stupid, Stafford!' Lady Anstey replied. "'Your wife is living in sin and you can easily divorce her!'

"'Which is something I have no intention of doing,' his Lordship answered, 'for the simple reason that I do not wish to wash my dirty linen in public'."

"'That may be all right for you,' Lady Anstey retorts, 'but what about me? I love you, Stafford, and I know you love me and we would be very happy together.'

"'I am sorry, Myrtle,' his Lordship says, 'We have discussed this before, and, although I am very grateful for the happiness you have given me, the answer is 'no'.'"

"He walks out from the room as he says that," Mrs. Hudson went on, "and I only just managed to move quickly away so that he wouldn't think I'd been listenin'."

"And Lady Anstey disappeared immediately after that?" Jaela asked.

"Oh, no, dear, it were three or four months later, after she'd been pleadin', beggin' and almost bullyin' his Lordship into marryin' her."

Jaela thought that it would be very difficult to bully the Earl into doing anything he did not want to do.

But she did not say so and Mrs. Hudson plunged on,

"Her Ladyship made it clear to everybody that she intended to marry him but Rose, who maided her, she's the niece of the porter's wife, told us she used to say,

"I will change that in the future! I will not have that sort of thing when I am living here!"

"She must have been very determined to have her own way," Jaela remarked.

"Oh, she were," Mrs. Hudson agreed. "And she often talked to the neighbours of how she and his Lordship were goin' to be married as soon as he were free."

Mrs. Hudson's story was now obviously at an end.

And Jaela said,

"And then she vanished?"

"Just disappeared into thin air," Mrs. Hudson replied. "If I'd not been here and seen it happen with me own eyes, I wouldn't have believed it."

"And they really looked everywhere for her?"

Mrs. Hudson lowered her voice again.

"I think, between ourselves, "that his Lordship thinks she committed suicide. He made them search everywhere and almost take The Castle to pieces brick by brick."

"It seems extraordinary," Jaela commented.

Mrs. Hudson glanced over her shoulder again.

"Of course," she said, "there were them as said that because she was so persistent, he'd done away with her."

"I cannot believe that is true!" Jaela exclaimed.

"Nor can I," Mrs. Hudson averred stoutly, "but they says it and 'twas impossible to stop them."

Jaela visualised all too clearly how the whispering about the Earl had started.

It was something he was powerless to prevent unless he could produce Lady Anstey or her body.

"It has aged him," Mrs. Hudson said sadly. "He were always reserved and 'buttoned into himself', if you knows what I mean, but after all that he were a different man in many ways."

"It is cruel what gossip can do," Jaela sighed.

"Of course he has his friends and his admirers," Mrs. Hudson went on as if she had not spoken. "That Mrs. Matherson, for one, dotes on him. She's a pretty woman and I can't help feelin' sorry for her."

"Why?" Jaela asked.

"Her husband, he were Master of the Fox Hounds, had an accident, three years ago it was."

"Was he badly injured?" Jaela asked.

"He broke his spine, my dear, and there were nothin' the doctors could do for him. He's in a wheelchair and 'tis hard on any woman to be nothin' but a nurse."

"Then that is another tragedy."

Jaela thought if it happened to her, she would rather be dead than a cripple for the rest of her life.

*

The following day Jaela was in the library with Kathy.

They were looking for books that had pictures of the places Jaela was describing to her.

They found one of the Coliseum in Rome and then one on the Harbour at Naples, which Kathy recognised.

She gave a delighted cry.

"I have been there with Mama," she said, "we got on a big ship that carried us and Uncle Diego to Africa."

As she spoke of the Conte, she remembered what Jaela had told her and looked over her shoulder.

"Papa is not here," she said, "so it is all right for me to talk about him to you?"

"Quite all right," Jaela agreed, "but now let's see if we can find some pictures of Paris, which we only passed through in the train."

She rose to look at the shelves and at that moment a woman came into the library.

She was smartly dressed and under her hat, which was trimmed with flowers, she had a very pretty face.

She was not beautiful as the Contessa had been but she was certainly very attractive.

She walked gracefully across the room with her eyes on Kathy.

"When I was told that you had returned, Katherine," she said, "I could hardly believe it. What a big girl you are. I am right in thinking that you must be eight years old, am I not?"

"I am eight," Kathy replied.

She caught Jaela's eye and dropped the newcomer a little curtsey.

"I am very pleased to know you, Katherine. My name is Matherson, Mrs. Matherson, and I am a very old friend of your father's."

Kathy did not reply.

Mrs. Matherson then turned her attention to Jaela.

It was obvious that she was surprised by the sight of her.

And after a moment she asked in a very different voice,

"Who are you? I do not seem to have met you before."

"I am Kathy's Governess," Jaela replied, "and my name is Compton."

"Her Governess?" Mrs. Matherson exclaimed.

There was an expression of relief in her eyes.

Then, as if it suddenly struck her, she said,

"You seem very young. I presume you were chosen for the position by her Ladyship."

"That is correct," Jaela replied coldly.

She thought it impertinent of Mrs. Matherson to ask her all these questions.

She had an instinctive feeling that Mrs. Matherson resented her being in The Castle.

"Do tell me," Mrs. Matherson said, "why Katherine has been sent to England in this unexpected manner. His Lordship said nothing about it to me."

Jaela did not answer and, with a little frown, Mrs. Matherson turned back to Kathy.

She was looking at the book that Jaela had just taken from the shelf.

"Tell me, dear child," she said in a honey-sweet voice, "how is your mother?"

"Mama is now with the angels," Kathy replied, "and, when I told her about my pony last night, she was very pleased I had one."

Mrs. Matherson stared at Kathy in astonishment.

Then she turned back to Jaela.

"What is the child saying?" she asked in a whisper. "That her mother is dead?"

"Yes, that is true," Jaela answered.

Mrs. Matherson drew in her breath.

"Now I understand!"

Without saying anything more she walked out of the library and along the passage to the Earl's study.

It was a beautiful room with long diamond-paned windows and the pictures on the wall were of horses. On his writing desk was an inkpot made from the foot of one of his favourite stallions and it had been encased in gold.

As Mrs. Matherson opened the door, the Earl, who was writing a letter, put down his pen and rose to his feet.

"Good morning, Sybil," he said. "I rather expected that you would come over."

Mrs. Matherson closed the door and ran across the room to him.

"Oh, Stafford," she said in an emotional voice, "I have just heard that your wife is dead."

"That is true," he replied, "but I did not know about it until after my daughter arrived."

"So that is why she carne back to you," Mrs. Matherson exclaimed. "I thought you must have asked her to come without telling me."

"No, of course not. I had no idea that she was arriving until she appeared."

Mrs. Matherson's hand tightened on his arm.

"So now you are free," she said softly. "Oh, darling Stafford, I am so glad."

As if he disliked the conversation, the Earl moved away from her.

He walked towards the fireplace to stand with his back to it.

Mrs. Matherson sat down very elegantly on the arm of a chair.

"The child is sweet and so pretty. I am sure you will be very proud of her. At the same time I should get rid of that theatrical-looking woman who says she is her Governess."

"She seems to be adequate," the Earl commented briefly.

"She is far too young to be the type of Governess you require for your daughter," Mrs. Matherson said, "and I will find you someone who is older and certainly a better teacher."

The Earl did not reply, but after a moment he asked,

"How is Edward?"

"Just the same," Mrs. Matherson said. "Very disagreeable, but he ever anything else?"

The Earl's rather hard expression softened.

"You know I am very sorry for you, Sybil."

"I am sorry for myself, but as long as I have you then I can bear this cross that has been laid on my shoulders."

The Earl frowned.

Then, as if he wished to change the subject, he asked her,

"Did you enjoy yourself in London?"

"I spent the entire time shopping," Sybil Matherson replied. "I was practically in rags, and you know that I want you to admire me."

As the Earl did not comment on this she added,

"I only came back late last night and, of course, have now driven over to see you only to be astonished when Whitlock told me that your daughter had returned unexpectedly."

"The trouble with Whitlock is that he always talks too much," the Earl remarked. "I was intending to see you this afternoon and tell you the news myself."

"Oh, darling, that will be lovely!" Sybil Matherson exclaimed. "At the same time I could not wait until this afternoon to see you."

The Earl's frown had by now deepened.

He walked across the room to the window to stand with his back to the room looking out at the colourful garden.

"What is the matter, Stafford?"

"I was just thinking," he said without turning, "that now my daughter is living here we must be more circumspect."

There was silence until Mrs. Matherson asked in an incredulous tone,

"Are you telling me and are you suggesting that we should not go on seeing each other?"

"No, of course not," the Earl replied hastily, "but I think it is a mistake for you to behave as you have recently as if you run The Castle and you come to me at night."

Sybil Matherson rose to her feet.

"Stafford, you must have gone mad," she cried. "You know as well as I do that, when I give Edward a sleeping draught, he knows nothing until the morning."

The Earl did not speak and she went on,

"None of your servants have the least idea that I enter The Castle by the side door in the Tower to reach your bedroom by the secret staircase."

The Earl moved restlessly and then walked back to the fireplace.

"You have been very kind to me, Sybil," he said, "and you know I have no wish to make you unhappy, but frankly

I want my daughter to forget the life she has led with her mother for the last six years."

Now there was a darkness in his eyes and an unmistakably angry note in his voice.

For a moment Sybil Matherson did not move. Then she drew in her breath and, as if she forced herself to speak gently, she said,

"Stafford, I love you. How can I live without you? How could I endure the misery and frustration of my life without your support and without your love?"

The Earl did not answer and she threw herself against him.

"I cannot lose you, Stafford," she murmured and her voice was now pathetic. "Please, *please* be kind to me."

The Earl looked down at her pleading eyes.

Very gently he put his hands on her shoulders and moved her away from him.

"It is something we have to think about, Sybil," he said, "and I must do what is right for my daughter."

Sybil Matherson drew a lace-edged handkerchief from the belt of her gown and wiped her eyes.

"I have never thought after we have meant so much to each other," she sighed, "that you would ever say anything like this to me."

"I know, I know!" the Earl said, "but Katherine is an intelligent child. She has for the last six years watched her mother living in sin. What is she going to think if she finds out that her father is behaving in exactly the same manner?"

Again he walked across the room to the window as if it was impossible to keep still.

As he did so, Sybil Matherson took the handkerchief from her eyes.

She stared at his dark head silhouetted against the sunshine and she was thinking that to make a scene would be a mistake.

In a brave little voice she stated,

"You know, dearest, all I want is your happiness and, although it will break my heart, I will do whatever you ask me to do."

The Earl heaved a sigh of relief.

"Thank you, Sybil," he said, "that is very generous and very like you. I knew you would not fail me."

Sybil Matherson clasped her fingers together.

"I have a feeling," she said softly, "that the Fates will be kinder than they are now and that somehow eventually we will be able to be together again and as happy as we have been in – the past."

Her voice broke dramatically on the last four words and then she rose.

"I was going to ask you to give me luncheon," she said, "but, as I expect you will have Katherine with you, I will go home."

"Thank you, Sybil," the Earl nodded.

She hesitated before she added,

"You would not like me to come to you tonight? No one would know and I have missed you so much while I have been in London."

There was a pause before the Earl replied,

"I think it would be a mistake."

Mrs. Matherson gave a little sob, but she did not protest.

She merely walked towards the door and, when she reached it, she looked back.

"Goodbye, Stafford," she said. "I love you and I shall be praying that we can be together in the not too distant future."

Before he could reply, she walked out of the study.

He could hear her footsteps as she went down the corridor.

Only when there was silence did the Earl take a handkerchief from his pocket and wiped his forehead.

It had been a difficult thing to do.

He knew of old just how hysterical a woman could be when he had ended an *affaire de coeur*.

Where Sybil Matherson was concerned, it was something that he had been wanting to do for quite some time.

But he had been unable to think of an excuse.

At least when he was not entertaining his friends she had relieved the loneliness of The Castle.

He had always been aware that he needed a woman to make it a real home.

He often thought that perhaps the cruellest thing that his wife had done when she left him was to take their baby with her.

When Katherine was born, he had wanted a son, of course, he had.

But there had been, he believed, plenty of time.

When his wife had decorated the nursery, he had seen to it that there was room for half-a-dozen children.

Then when she left him, he had been honest enough to realise that it was really his own fault.

Before his marriage he had always been with endless sophisticated, witty and amusing women who went out of their way to attract and amuse him.

They were all experienced in kindling the fires of desire in a man from the first moment they met him.

Anne had been extremely lovely.

She was also as well-born as he was himself and her father was a very rich man.

At twenty-three his large number of relations were already pestering him to produce an heir to the Earldom and all the treasures of The Castle.

He had in fact thought that Anne was exactly all that he desired in a wife.

It was only when they were married that he was shocked.

Like most young girls in the Social world, Anne was extremely badly educated.

Her conversation was little more, he felt scornfully, than what he would have expected of a dairy maid.

She had suffered very considerably from sickness when she was expecting her baby and it was therefore almost impossible for him not to drift into being unfaithful to her.

He went to London and she stayed behind at The Castle.

After Katherine was born, Anne was far more interested in the baby than she was in him.

He found then that neither his horses nor the problems of his estate were enough to fill his days.

So he drifted back to London and there were any number of beautiful women with open arms waiting to embrace him warmly.

He had had no idea until very much later that quite by chance Anne had met the Conte di Agnolo.

It was at a party given by the Lord Lieutenant and some Diplomats had been invited.

The Conte had heard of the Earl's horses and had asked Anne if it was possible for him to see them and he visited The Castle on the following day to inspect them.

That was just the beginning.

As there was no sign of her husband returning from London, Anne had invited the Conte to stay at The Castle.

He rode the horses that he so greatly admired and she naturally invited a number of her friends to meet him.

The Conte made the party one of the most amusing that Anne had ever known.

They laughed, they talked and they sang songs round the piano.

Every Italian is musical, every Italian is romantic and no one missed the Earl.

When they went to bed after the first evening, Anne thought that she had never enjoyed herself more.

The Conte's compliments had made her blush and, for the very first time since she had married, the conversation had not been about horses.

Every word spoken seemed to sparkle like jewels and Anne thought of several things to say that her friends thought were witty and original.

The open admiration in the Conte's eyes was very encouraging.

She had originally asked him to stay for two days, but he had stayed for a whole week.

Then he asked if he could return in two months' time as he was coming to England on a mission that concerned the Italian Government.

The Earl duly came back from London.

He had no idea that his wife was counting the days until the Conte di Agnolo would be their guest.

It happened to coincide with the racing at Newmarket.

So he told Anne that she must have her party without him, while once again the Earl was very successful on the Racecourse.

By the time he returned home from Newmarket, his wife, although he did not notice it, was a changed person.

Now she wanted to go to London.

Not for the same reason that he did, but because she wanted to buy new clothes.

Clothes that the Conte, when he came again from Italy, would admire her in.

Anne and the Conte met in London, staying in a house party given by some friends of his and the hostess was Italian and very understanding.

When Anne went back to The Castle, she was beginning to think of it as a prison rather than a home.

The Earl at the time had become involved in a fiery *affaire de coeur* with the Russian Ambassador's wife.

She was very demanding and he found it difficult not to spend a great deal more time than he intended in her company.

There was inevitably a so-called 'friend' who warned Anne that her husband was being unfaithful.

It did not hurt her, it merely swept away her last feelings of guilt, which had prevented her from giving in very much earlier to the Conte's pleadings.

She was wildly, passionately and overwhelmingly in love and so only the thought of his Italian family had held her back.

Now she knew that she was unable to resist him.

She had loved him from the first moment that he had kissed her.

When she found out about the Earl, she felt that it opened the door to her freedom.

When she told the Conte that she could no longer live without him, he therefore arranged everything.

At the last moment, she went into the pale pink nursery.

Katherine was lying in her cot and the fair hair that now covered her head was entirely of curls.

She was exactly, Anne thought, like a small angel and she could not bear to think of her being lonely or neglected when her father was constantly away with his Russian mistress.

There would only be the servants in The Castle to look after her.

Anne's luggage was already piled onto the carriage that was to take her to the Halt.

And there she would board the train for London.

As Anne came down the steps of The Castle, she was carrying Katherine in her arms.

Whitlock stared at her in astonishment.

"You're takin' the baby with you, my Lady?"

"I am, Whitlock, and Rose is coming with me as far as London."

Whitlock did not ask the Countess where she was going and he waited for Rose to return and tell him where her Ladyship had gone.

Rose informed him that the Countess had not stayed at Hale House as she had assumed she would.

A carriage had been waiting for them at the Station.

"The Conte was so surprised to see the baby," Rose recounted.

Then the Countess had said,

"Goodbye, Rose, and thank you very much for coming with me. Now you must take a Hackney carriage to Hale House, stay the night and they will provide you with your ticket to go back to The Castle."

"Before I could catch me breath," Rose had then related, "'Er Ladyship had got into the carriage and driven off."

After that no one had seen her again.

Only when the Earl returned home and was mystified by her disappearance did a letter arrive.

The servants, recognising her Ladyship's handwriting, knew that it was ominous.

They were not surprised when the Earl carried it into his study and closed the door.

For two hours no one dared disturb him and, when he did come out, there was a grimness about his expression that made the young footmen tremble.

He had gone riding until it was dark and, when he returned, his horse was sweating and on the point of exhaustion.

Whitlock waited on his Lordship at dinner and he never spoke a word and for the next few days the whole Castle seemed to be shrouded in heavy gloom.

And then the Earl went back to London and did not return for over a month.

When he did, he announced that the Countess was ill and the doctors had ordered her to live in a warmer climate.

He did not say where she was and nor did he mention his daughter, Katherine.

It was only when the winter came and the Earl's friends came to stay for the hunting that things looked better.

"Things is gettin' back to normal," Mrs. Hudson had said to Whitlock.

"Things ain't normal if a young man like his Lordship be without a woman," he replied.

*

When Mrs. Matherson had left the library, Jaela quickly found the books that she wanted for Kathy.

She took the child upstairs to the schoolroom.

She had an instinct about other people that she had developed with her father and she felt very strongly that the pretty woman intended to make trouble.

As Kathy played on the floor with Rufus, she looked into the mirror.

She told herself that a sensible older woman in point of fact would be more suitable as a Governess.

If, as she suspected, Mrs. Matherson was infatuated with the Earl, she would try to get rid of her.

'I am too young and too pretty,' she told her reflection.

But she was sure that the Earl was far too proud and too conscious of his own importance to become involved with anyone he employed.

She was a Governess who after all was only a senior servant.

Not that she wished to be involved with him in any way.

She did, however, find him most interesting because he was so different in every way from any man she had met before.

She saw in him a likeness to her father, but perhaps that was because both of them were English.

'I wonder if he is clever?' she questioned.

There were a great number of books in the library, but that proved nothing.

She had not had a chance of any conversation with the Earl.

It was therefore difficult to know if there were any brains behind that handsome cynical face.

Almost as if her question was answered by Fate, when the footman brought up her dinner he said,

"'Is Lordship's compliments, miss, and 'e'd like to see you in 'is study at eight-forty-five after dinner."

It was what Jaela had been expecting.

She had felt very certain that sooner or later the Earl would question her ability to teach Kathy.

Automatically, as she had always done so, she had bathed and changed before dinner.

Her gowns were all pretty and expensive-looking and she put on one that she had bought in Naples.

It was actually one of her father's favourites.

It was white because he liked her to look young and like a *debutante*, but there were little bunches of musk roses on the skirt and on the puffed sleeves.

The neck was, she thought, somewhat low for a Governess.

Yet she had not expected to see anyone except for the footmen and she wondered now if she should change again.

Then the question was what else could she wear?

She revolted against the idea of appearing in her day clothes.

She had changed for dinner as she had done ever since she was old enough to dine with her father and mother.

Then she laughed at her own concern.

She was quite certain that the Earl would not take the slightest interest in anything but her ability as a teacher.

He had certainly made that clear up until now.

The sharpness of his orders and the way he found fault showed that he thought her rather stupid.

She went downstairs at exactly eight-forty-five.

She held her head high and actually felt somewhat aggressive.

By doubting her ability to teach a small child of eight, the Earl was insulting not her but her father.

His brilliance had been acclaimed the whole length and breadth of the country.

The Earl was waiting for her in the study, standing with his back to the fireplace.

She had the feeling that, if he had not been standing, he would not have risen when she walked towards him.

She thought too that he was surprised when he looked at her.

She curtseyed and then waited for his permission to sit down.

"You are looking very smart, Miss Compton," he said. "Have you changed into your best because I sent for you?"

The way he spoke made Jaela feel angry.

"No, my Lord," she said coldly, "I had already bathed and changed before I had received your summons. I can only apologise therefore if my gown gives offence."

"It does not do that," the Earl replied, "it only seems to me to be more suitable for a ball than a schoolroom."

"Then I must, of course, obey your Lordship's wishes and I will buy something in the local market that will not displease you."

She spoke spontaneously.

Then she wondered if she had been too rude and the Earl would then dismiss her.

Instead he laughed.

"What you wear is immaterial, Miss Compton. What I wish to discuss with you is my daughter's education."

"I expected you would wish to do that, my Lord, and may I inform you that Kathy is an extremely intelligent child and very easy to teach?"

She saw that he was listening to her intently and went on,

"She already speaks Italian and French and I shall take care that she does not forget these languages. It certainly makes it easier to teach her Geography – and History does not confine itself to the British Isles."

The Earl then crossed his legs and looked, Jaela thought, very Regal in his high-backed armchair.

"From what you say, Miss Compton," he said after a moment, "I have the impression that you yourself have travelled quite considerably."

"I have been to most countries in Europe," Jaela replied.

"I find that difficult to credit, when you look so young," the Earl remarked at once.

Jaela did not answer, she merely sat upright, her hands in her lap.

She was thinking that, if he was so determined to be difficult, she would not let him get away with it.

There was silence until the Earl persisted,

"Well? Have you nothing to say about that?"

"I thought, my Lord, what we were discussing was how I was to teach Kathy."

"Then suppose you tell me what you are teaching her already?"

"She has had an Arithmetic lesson this morning in the three languages she speaks."

"How is that possible?" the Earl asked.

"We 'went shopping' this morning round one of your rooms," Jaela answered, "in which there are many *objets d'art*. First we bought presents in Italian, while Kathy counted what the gifts came to and how much she would have to pay for them in Italian lire."

Jaela paused, then went on,

"After that we did the same in French francs and then in English pounds, shillings and pence."

The Earl stared at her and then he commented,

"You are certainly original, Miss Compton!"

He did not make it sound exactly like a compliment.

Jaela remained silent.

"And what other lessons are you planning for my daughter?"

"She is musical," Jaela answered, "and she loves stories of every sort and description, which makes Literature a very interesting subject for her. And I think the best way to teach her Geography would be for her to collect stamps."

The Earl started and then he queried,

"Who has been talking to you?"

"Talking to me?" Jaela enquired.

"About my interest?"

She stared at him and then she said,

"If you are a stamp collector, my Lord, I certainly had no idea of it."

The Earl rose to his feet and, walking to a drawer in his desk, drew out a book.

He opened it and then held it out to Jaela.

For a moment she just looked at the page.

Then she exclaimed,

"You have a 'Penny Black'! You must be very proud. I remember how excited my father was when he found one."

"Are you saying that your father collected stamps?"

Jaela rose to her feet.

"I have something to show Your Lordship that I think will really interest you."

She did not wait for his permission, but then ran from the room and up the stairs to her bedroom.

She had left the heavy trunks that contained her father's books and some other personal possessions at Mellor House in London.

But two albums of his stamp collection were in the bottom of one of the trunks that she had brought with her.

She had actually been looking at them the night before she had left for England and she had put those two books into the luggage she wanted on the train and she had not bothered to unpack them when she was in London.

She picked them up now and ran back down the stairs with them under her arm.

The Earl was waiting for her and now he was looking amused.

"If your stamps are very much better than mine, Miss Compton," he said, "I shall then be extremely annoyed. I have been collecting them ever since I was a small boy and none of my contemporaries who did the same has a better collection."

Jaela did not answer, she merely opened the first of her father's albums.

He had collected stamps since he was a young man and he had the distinct advantage of the finest stamps, which came on letters to his Chambers and to the House of Lords.

The Earl saw first a Penny Black, which was in an even better condition than his own.

Then he could see the Brazil Bulls Eye, the first stamp issued in 1843 in the Western Hemisphere.

He gave an audible gasp.

He put the book down on his desk to turn the pages over one by one.

"I don't believe it," he said aloud. "It is the most amazing collection I have ever seen! I suppose, Miss Compton, you are aware that it is very valuable?"

"I would not sell it, my Lord, for all the gold in the world." Jaela admitted quietly.

"But if you did do so, you would not have to work for your living," the Earl remarked.

She did not answer and he looked up at her.

She had the feeling that his eyes were boring beneath the surface.

"I suppose you *do* have to work for your living?" he next asked her slowly.

CHAPTER FIVE

There was a silence and then Jaela said,

"You have not yet seen the second book of my father's stamps, my Lord."

The Earl smiled.

"In other words, you are telling me to mind my own business."

"I think, my Lord," Jaela retorted, "we were talking about Kathy and, of course, stamp collecting as well, which is more important."

"I agree with you," the Earl said, "and I apologise for diverting from the text."

There was a sarcastic note in his voice, which she did not miss.

Instead she handed the second of her father's albums to him saying,

"I hope your Lordship will not be envious, but I am very certain that you cannot equal the stamp on the first page."

The Earl took the album from her and opened it cautiously.

Then he exclaimed,

"I don't believe it! The British Guyana One Penny Magenta is the most valuable stamp in the world!"

"That is what my father always said and he was very fortunate to have obtained it."

Jaela did not add that Lord Compton had received the stamp, which was issued in 1856, as an expression of gratitude when he was at the Bar from a Guyanian whom he had saved from being hanged when he was accused of murder.

The Earl was staring at the stamp as if he could hardly believe his eyes.

Then he said,

"You are very fortunate, Miss Compton, and I suppose it would be quite useless for me to offer you almost any sum you wish for this particular stamp."

Jaela shook her head.

"To me my father's collection is a memento of all the happiness we shared together and while one day I might give it to somebody I love, I would never part with it for money."

"I understand what you are saying," the Earl replied, "and I can only congratulate you and, of course, beg you to be very careful not to leave your collection lying about in case it is stolen."

"In the Castle?" Jaela queried. "I think that is unlikely."

"I am not thinking of it being insecure whilst you are here," the Earl replied, "but when you leave us."

Jaela was still.

"You – you are not – suggesting that might be soon?" she asked in a low voice.

As she spoke, she recognised that to leave Kathy in The Castle would at this moment be unbearable.

The Earl was watching the expression on her face, and after a few moments he enquired,

"You like being here, Miss Compton? You are happy?"

"Very happy, my Lord."

"It seems to me extraordinary that anyone so young and so lovely should be content with looking after a small child," he said, "rather than having a number of admirers at her feet."

He spoke seriously, but Jaela laughed and replied,

"That, in point of fact, is the last thing I want."

Then, as if she felt that she must explain to the Earl, although why she should do so she had no idea, she said in a very different tone,

"I am actually in mourning and, just as Kathy has to face a new world, one of which she knows very little about, I am doing the same."

"Then shall I say," the Earl answered, "that, as a part of your new world, I will do my best to make it pleasant both for Kathy and for you."

Jaela smiled at him and she had no idea how enchanting she looked as she did so.

Her smile was not only on her lips but also in her eyes.

"I want to stay here," she said. "I find it all very exciting and, although you may think it presumptuous, Kathy has crept into my heart and I have no wish to leave her."

"She is certainly a very attractive child," the Earl said, "and I am sure that your idea of teaching her Geography from stamps is a good one. I am just wondering if there are enough of them in the world as yet."

"In the last issue of the Mount Brown catalogue that my father had received," Jaela said, "there were two thousand four hundred stamps listed and, as it was published in 1866, there must be a great many more by now."

"All right, Miss Compton, you win," the Earl said. "I am sure you are correct in thinking that more and more countries will issue stamps so, of course, I must obtain them both for my own collection and for yours."

"That would be very kind of you," Jaela responded, "because although it was my father's special hobby stamps have always fascinated me."

"Well, now we must make sure that they fascinate Katherine," the Earl suggested.

"Of course."

He began to turn over the pages of Lord Compton's album.

Every so often he made an exclamation when he found some particular stamp that was of great importance and which he did not own himself.

There was the 'Basil Dove' from Switzerland ,which had been issued in 1848. Also the first pictorial stamp of New South Wales, which was issued in 1850.

They went on talking and discussing the stamps from different places until Jaela realised to her astonishment that it was nearly midnight.

She rose to her feet saying,

"I must apologise for keeping your Lordship up so late. I had no idea of the time."

"Nor had I," the Earl answered.

He looked again at Lord Compton's album as if he could hardly bear to part with it.

Then he said,

"Tomorrow I will write to London to Stanley Gibbons and ask him for his catalogue and find out when the next sales are taking place. When I do, I promise to be an eager bidder."

Jaela clasped her hands together.

"It is so exciting to think I can go on with Papa's collection. I was sticking in the last stamps he had bought when Dr. Pirelli arrived at the Villa to ask me to go to England."

As she spoke, she realised that she had inadvertently revealed to the Earl that she was living in Italy in a different Villa from that occupied by Kathy and her mother.

She knew by the expression in his eyes that what she had said had not gone unnoticed.

He did not say anything, but merely handed her her father's albums.

"I hope that you will allow me to study these another evening," he said, "and I shall be anxious to know exactly what you are teaching Katherine about the countries that they come from."

As Jaela took the albums from him, he added,

"Of course, I will try to believe that you are telling me the truth when you tell me that you have visited every one of them!"

Jaela laughed.

"I would not lie to your Lordship, but I have in fact travelled quite a lot, so I have plenty of stories to tell Kathy about the people, their customs and their costumes."

"I am *trying* to believe you, Miss Compton," the Earl remarked.

She knew that now he was not being sarcastic but merely teasing her.

She dropped him a graceful curtsey and said,

"Goodnight, my Lord, and thank you for what has been an exciting, I might almost say an enchanted evening."

Only as she left the study did she wonder if she had been too effusive.

It was not the correct way for an ordinary Governess to speak to her employer.

But she had been speaking to him not as a Governess but as one philatelist to another.

He was almost as fanatical about stamps and their history as her father had been.

'How could I have imagined,' she asked herself as she went into the nursery, 'that in England I would find a sportsman as keen as Papa on a very specialised and unusual subject?'

When she went to bed, she thought a little anxiously that she had undoubtedly made the Earl curious about her.

It had been impossible when they were talking not to say occasionally how her father had obtained some particular stamp.

It often had been with the help either of the British Embassy or else of some particular Ministry in the country where it had been issued.

Thinking back, she knew that it would have been impossible for an ordinary collector to obtain such stamps.

She was certain that the Earl was aware of this.

'I must be more careful,' she admonished herself, 'for if I reveal who I am, I shall not be able to stay on in The Castle.'

It would certainly be unconventional to say the least for the daughter of Lord Compton of Mellor to be there alone with the Earl of Halesworth.

A Governess, being of no social standing, could live there as an employee, but then she herself would have to have a married woman to chaperone her.

'I must be careful – *very careful!*'

Jaela was saying the words over and over to herself as she fell asleep.

*

The next morning before Jaela went riding with Kathy she had learnt that the Earl would be away from The Castle all day.

She therefore thought that it would be a good idea to take Kathy exploring.

The State Rooms were very impressive, although the shutters were closed over some of the windows and she learnt from Whitlock that they had not been used for some time.

The old Tower was fascinating.

They climbed up twisting narrow stone steps to stand at the top from where there was a magnificent view.

Jaela told Kathy how this Castle as well as many others in the East of England had been built to guard against the Danes who invaded England frequently from across the North Sea.

Kathy found this thrilling.

She wanted to know how many soldiers had kept watch in the Tower and what the Danes stole from the land.

She was so curious that Jaela thought that she would have to find a History book on the subject.

"We will go and search for one in the library," she told Kathy.

However when they did, they found so many interesting books on the shelves that for the moment the invading Danes were forgotten.

Late that night when Jaela was in bed she heard the Earl return and wondered where he had been.

Maybe he had been visiting some lovely lady in the neighbourhood. It was certainly what Mrs. Hudson would have expected him to do.

Then she told herself that it was a mistake for her to become too interested in the Earl and what he did or did not do.

She had at first thought him arrogant and somewhat aggressive.

Yet, when he was talking about stamps, he had been so very human and she had changed her opinion of him.

'He has certainly been kind to Kathy,' she mused.

She remembered how horrifying it had been when they had first arrived and he had told her to take Kathy back to where she had come from.

Even now she could remember the harshness in his voice and she had felt as if he had struck her because it had been so intimidating.

'Now everything has changed,' she thought to herself happily.

When she had kissed Kathy goodnight, Rufus was curled up at the bottom of her bed.

She had put her arms around the child saying,

"Goodnight, darling. We will go riding tomorrow morning if it is a nice day."

"Today was a lovely one," Kathy said, "I rode on Snowball, I explored The Castle and climbed up that big high Tower."

There was a rapt note in her voice that told Jaela how much it had meant to her.

"You are very fortunate to have such an exciting home," she said.

"With lots and lots of stories in it," Kathy then added, "and I love you, Miss Compton, because you tell me such thrilling stories."

Jaela blew out the candle and then, as she reached the door, she said, as her mother had said to her when she was Kathy's age,

"Goodnight, darling, and may the angels guard over you until the morrow."

Now in the darkness Jaela said to her father and mother,

'I believe that both you and the angels are guarding me all the time.'

*

The Earl was getting ready to go riding as he usually did before breakfast.

There was a knock on the door which his valet answered.

"This has just arrived for 'is Lordship," a footman said.

He handed the valet a note on a silver salver and the man took it to the Earl.

He recognised the handwriting and there was a frown between his eyes as he walked to the window to open it.

He thought it was indiscreet of Sybil Matherson to send him a note so early in the day.

Then, as he took the sheet of writing paper out of the envelope, he stared down at what she had written,

"*Dearest Stafford,*

Edward died last night and I feel helpless to cope with the shock of it and with everything that must be done.

Please come and help me. You are the only person I can rely on and I am all alone.

Sybil."

The Earl read it through slowly and then read it again. He knew that it was a cry for help that he could not ignore.

At the same time he thought that it was not right for Sybil to make him responsible for her.

He turned from the window and saw that his valet was holding in his hand his whipcord jacket which he wore when out riding.

He hesitated for a few moments and then he said,

"Order my curricle with two horses and I will change into my driving clothes."

"Very good, my Lord."

The valet hurried from the room to give the order and then he came back to assist his Master.

Twenty minutes later the Earl left The Castle.

But instead of going directly to Matherson House, which was about two miles away, he went a mile or so in the opposite direction.

He drove through a small village where at the end of it was an attractive Manor House occupied by one of his relatives.

Colonel Worth had been in the Grenadiers before he retired and his wife was a charming woman of nearly sixty.

She was out in the garden and was already tending her many plants.

The Earl came across the lawn towards her.

"Stafford!" she exclaimed as he reached her. "It is a considerable surprise to see you, but a very pleasant one."

The Earl kissed her cheek and then he said,

"I am afraid, Elizabeth, I have bad news and I need your help."

Elizabeth Worth looked at him anxiously.

"What has happened?" she enquired.

"Edward Matherson died last night and I want you to come with me to see if we can be of some help to Sybil."

"He has died?" Mrs. Worth exclaimed. "Poor man! He has suffered so very much since he broke his spine. But he was so strong that I thought that he would live for many more years."

"So did I," the Earl replied, "but I have had a note from Sybil and she sounds somewhat distraught."

"It is hardly surprising," Mrs. Worth said, "and, of course, I will come with you at once. I am afraid Henry has gone riding, but the servants will tell him what has happened and he will join us as soon as he gets back."

"That would be an excellent idea," the Earl agreed.

He waited in the comfortable sitting room where there was a picture of his cousin in full Regimental dress, and wearing his medals, over the mantelpiece.

Mrs. Worth did not take long.

As soon as she came down the stairs and climbed into the curricle, the Earl drove back the way he had come and then on to the Matherson house.

Edward Matherson had been the only son of Sir Roger Matherson who was the seventh Baronet.

The Earl was well aware that a great number of the family lived in the County or not far outside it.

He realised, when he had received Sybil's note, that it would be a great mistake to let them find him in charge when they arrived.

He could not help feeling that Sybil was pushing him into a responsible position and it was one that he had no intention of fulfilling.

When he arrived, he was certain that this was what she had planned.

He saw the expression in her eyes when she could see that he had brought Elizabeth with him.

"My dear Sybil!" Mrs. Worth said. "I am so very sorry for you and, of course, Henry and I will help you in any way we possibly can."

"I certainly need help," Sybil Matherson replied, but she was looking directly at the Earl as she spoke.

Not entirely to the Earl's surprise, he found that she had not notified anyone else of her husband's death.

Accordingly, while Elizabeth Worth was talking to Sybil, he went to the stables.

He sent grooms off in every direction to inform Edward Matherson's relatives what had happened.

When he returned to the house, he was glad to see a horse outside and he knew that it belonged to his Cousin, Henry Worth.

*

Later in the day the Earl left Sybil surrounded by a great number of Mathersons.

When he learnt that Sir Roger would be arriving later in the afternoon, he took Elizabeth Worth home again.

He had not had a private conversation with Sybil, but he was, however, well aware that she was trying to manoeuvre him into it.

Her husband, whom she had not cared for since he was injured, was only just dead.

Yet he was sure that she would be doing everything possible to renew their association.

The Earl had experienced so many dramatic scenes of tears and pleadings with so many different women.

He was determined therefore not to be involved again with Sybil, however hard she tried to put back the clock.

He thought, too late, that he should not have become involved with her in the first place.

But she had been very persistent and, as she did live so near to The Castle, it was just impossible to prevent her from continually popping in.

He now admitted to himself that he had found her attractive.

But it was simply because there had been no competition and he often felt lonely.

When he was in London, it was different.

There were old friends there to welcome him and there were always new and attractive beauties and they made it very obvious that they found him irresistible.

Sometimes, when he sat alone in the study with the wind howling round the walls of The Castle, he had a longing for something warm and soft to hold in his arms.

So it had been difficult to resist Sybil.

She had discovered just how easily she was able to enter The Castle at the bottom of the Tower and from there she would creep up a secret passage which must have been used by many generations to the first floor.

There was no one at that time of the night to notice a horse left tethered to the railings.

The Earl was well aware, although he did not like to think about it, that she had given her husband a sleeping draught of laudanum.

He had therefore no idea the morning that she had not been in the next room all night.

'It was a great mistake,' the Earl accused himself now.

When he reached Elizabeth Worth's house, he said,

"Thank you, Elizabeth. It was very kind of you to come with me. I am sure that Sybil very much appreciated it."

"I think, Stafford, she would rather have had you alone," Elizabeth Worth said frankly. "And forgive me if I am being impertinent, but are you thinking of marrying her now that she is free?"

"Certainly not!" the Earl replied. "I have no intention, Elizabeth, of marrying anyone and that is the truth!"

"I believe you, Stafford," Mrs. Worth said. "At the same time Sybil hinted to me when we were alone that you had a great fondness for each other."

The Earl's lips tightened and there was an expression in his eyes that made Elizabeth Worth say quickly,

"Perhaps I should not have told you, but you know, Stafford dear, we would all be very glad if you found somebody who could make you happy."

He did not speak and she continued,

"And, of course, it would be wonderful for Kathy to have some brothers and sisters to play with."

The Earl stiffened.

Then he smiled a little wryly.

"You were always very outspoken, Elizabeth," he said, "And I understand that you are speaking for my own good. But will you please make it clear to anyone who is interested that I am not in love with Sybil Matherson."

His voice deepened as he added,

"I am for the moment concerned only with the happiness of my daughter, who has come back to me after being away for so long."

Elizabeth Worth put her hand on his arm.

"I understand, Stafford dear. It is really your own fault for being so handsome, but I will certainly do what you ask of me."

"Thank you," the Earl said.

He kissed her and then drove back to The Castle.

He found, when he walked into the hall, that the news had already reached the staff.

"We've heard about Mr. Matherson, my Lord," Whitlock said, "And it be sad news, very sad. But one can't help thinkin', seein' the condition the poor gentleman were in, that it's a merciful release."

"That is what I think too," the Earl replied and walked towards his study.

*

That night the Earl did not send for Jaela and she felt disappointed.

Although she laughed at herself for doing so, she had put on one of her prettiest gowns and she had arranged her hair in what she thought was a new and fashionable style.

She put her father's albums lying ready on a table in the nursery.

But there was no call from downstairs.

She thought that she was being presumptuous in thinking that there might have been and she could not help wondering what the Earl was feeling about the death of Mr. Matherson.

His wife was now free and the Earl was free too.

They would have to wait a year and, when the time of mourning was over, they could be married.

She hoped, however, that he would not do so.

She had the feeling, and it was a very strong one, that Sybil Matherson would not make a particularly good mother for Kathy.

She looked in on the child last thing at night before she went to her own bedroom.

Kathy was fast asleep.

Curled up beside her with his head almost on the pillow was Rufus.

It was something Jaela was aware that she should not allow.

At the same time she recognised just much Kathy loved the dog and it was Rufus and Snowball who had prevented her from being very upset at her mother's death.

'The child wants love,' she told herself.

Almost as if somebody asked the question, she seemed to hear a voice saying,

'That is what the Earl wants and what you want too!'

Jaela closed Kathy's door gently and went to her own room.

When she was in bed, she thought about the Earl.

For six years he had been without a wife.

Of course there had been women in his life, but it was not the same as having a wife and children to fill The Castle.

'I am very sorry for him,' she finally admitted to herself.

She realised it was something that she had never expected to feel about someone quite so important.

Most people would think that he had everything in the world to make him happy.

'No one is ever happy without love,' she reasoned in the same way that she might have talked to her father.

It was love that had made the Countess run away with the Conte, who had really loved her.

It was love which had made her send her daughter home to where she belonged.

And now Kathy was at her home to stay.

Jaela had a sudden terrifying feeling that she might be made unhappy by a woman who loved her father but not her.

'She would be jealous of another woman's child,' she told herself, 'and jealous too if the Earl gave his child the attention she thought should be lavished on her and her children.'

Nothing had happened yet.

Yet she felt as if she had to stand like a sentinel between Kathy and the whole world.

'There is nothing I can do,' she reasoned logically.

At the same time she knew that she could not shrug off all responsibility for her.

It was what she had undertaken when the Contessa has asked her to look after Kathy.

'I will try, *I will try*!' she vowed in her heart.

At the same time she was afraid.

She knew as well that she had an almost clairvoyant premonition that there was disaster ahead.

When it was to happen exactly she did not know.

Yet her intuition and her perception had always been very acute.

She felt now as if she was in a runaway train that was carrying her down a steep incline to disaster.

'I am being imaginative and very foolish!' she scolded herself.

She turned from side to side.

Yet she could not escape from the idea that something terrible was going to happen.

She felt as if, dark and frightening, it was coming down from the ceiling and would drop on her so that she could not escape from it.

'I am having a nightmare,' she told herself.

But she was not asleep.

Then, as if her father was near her, she whispered,
'I am afraid, Papa! Help me! Watch over me.'

CHAPTER SIX

Jaela and Kathy came back from riding.

Because it was a nice day they had ridden rather further than usual.

They the took their horses to the stables.

And Kathy made a great fuss of Snowball before he was taken away into his stall.

She had been riding now without a leading-rein, which had delighted her and Jaela felt that she was becoming quite a good little horsewoman.

'It will please the Earl,' she thought, knowing how superb he was on a horse.

Hand-in-hand, with Kathy chattering excitedly, they went into The Castle.

When they reached the hall and were going upstairs to the nursery, the Earl came out of his study.

"I want you, Katherine," he called out.

She ran towards him, holding out her arms.

"I have had a lovely ride, Papa, and Miss Compton says I am getting better and better and I will soon be able to beat you."

The Earl laughed.

"High praise indeed," he said looking at Jaela.

"She really is very good," Jaela added quietly.

"What I have to ask you, Katherine," the Earl said to his daughter, "is if you will let me borrow Rufus for the day."

"Why, Papa?"

"I am taking him to see a very attractive lady dog from whom a friend of mine wishes to breed."

He was choosing his words carefully, Jaela realised, as he went on,

"I am offering her the choice of my two spaniels and Rufus as a husband and when she has puppies, I shall have the pick of the litters and whichever I choose will be yours!"

He had spoken slowly, so that Kathy could understand.

Now she gave a cry of joy.

"A puppy all for me? Oh, Papa, that would be fabulous."

Then she looked down at Rufus and said,

"But I will never love it more than Rufus. He is mine and the most wonderful dog in the whole wide world."

She bent down as she spoke to pat him and he jumped up at her eagerly.

She looked very pretty as she did so and Jaela saw a tender expression in the Earl's eyes that she had not seen there before.

'He is beginning to love the child as I do,' she mused.

"May I take Rufus with me?" the Earl asked.

"Yes, of course, Papa," Kathy agreed, "but be very very careful with him."

"You know I will," the Earl answered and Kathy bent to hug Rufus again and say to him,

"Now you are to go with Papa and be a very good boy otherwise I shall scold you when you come back."

Rufus appeared to understand.

When the Earl started to walk to the front door with the two other spaniels, he whistled to him.

Rufus looked at Kathy as if for permission.

"Go with Papa," Kathy said, "and be a good dog."

The Earl whistled again and Rufus followed him out through the front door.

Jaela took Kathy by the hand.

"Now we have to do some lessons," she began, "and today, as you are interested in the Danes, I thought that we would read what England was like when they invaded us with their Viking ships centuries ago."

"That will be very exciting," Kathy enthused as they went up the stairs.

Jaela had collected quite a number of History books from the library.

There were pictures of the Vikings and of the English and she also had a map on which she could point out the many places on the coast where they had landed.

Kathy was so absorbed that neither she nor Jaela were in any way aware that it was time for luncheon until their food came up.

When the Earl was at home without any guests, they ate with him in the dining room and when he was out a footman brought their luncheon upstairs.

When they had finished, Kathy looked out of the window and exclaimed,

"Oh, it is raining, Miss Compton, and I did so want to play in the garden."

Jaela walked to the window and saw that the child was right. It was raining quite hard and it might be just a short storm, but she thought that they were more probably in for a wet afternoon.

"I think we had better have another lesson," she said, "then tomorrow if it is a nice day we can stay out much longer."

For a moment Kathy did not speak and Jaela realised that she was disappointed.

Then she said,

"Tomorrow I will have Rufus with me and that will be more fun."

"Yes, of course, it will," Jaela agreed, "and I think because I know you love it, we will now have a music lesson."

Kathy's eyes lit up.

She liked to hear Jaela playing the piano and she was learning a special piece to play to her father once it was perfected.

There was an upright piano in one of the corners of the nursery.

Jaela had just sat down when to her surprise the door opened and Mrs. Matherson came in.

"I thought that you would be here, Katherine," Mrs. Matherson exclaimed, "and I have something very exciting to tell you!"

"What is it?" Kathy asked.

"It is something that I know will thrill you," Mrs. Matherson answered.

Kathy was listening to her and Jaela had risen politely from the music stool.

Mrs. Matherson was dressed in black and it was very becoming to her fair hair and blue eyes.

She sat down on a low chair.

She then held Kathy by the hand, and said,

"I don't know whether you realise it, but I am writing a book about The Castle and what it was like in the old days."

"I was just learning about that," Kathy said. "Will your book have pictures?"

"I hope so," Mrs. Matherson replied. "I came over here today to be quite certain that my description of the Tower was correct and what do you think I found?"

"What?" Kathy asked.

"A secret passage, which I am sure that no one, not even your father, has found before."

"A secret passage?" Kathy exclaimed. "How exciting!"

"That is what I thought," Mrs. Matherson said. "I hear that your father is out so perhaps you would like to see it first before anybody else does."

"I would love that," Kathy smiled.

"Then come along and I will show it to you," Mrs. Matherson proposed.

She rose and took Kathy by the hand.

Jaela, who had been listening, moved forward before they reached the door.

"I hope, Mrs. Matherson, I can come too," she said.

Mrs. Matherson hesitated and it seemed as if she had not thought of it.

Then before she could speak Kathy said,

"Miss Compton must come. She has been telling me all about the Danes and how the English watched for them from the Tower and shot them down with their arrows."

Mrs. Matherson smiled.

"Then, of course, Miss Compton must come with us."

So Jaela opened the door and Mrs. Matherson, still holding Kathy by the hand, went out first.

Jaela followed behind them.

She thought it strange that Mrs. Matherson should be so interested in The Castle.

Even if she was engaged in writing a book about it when she had not yet even buried her husband.

She had heard that the funeral would take place in two days' time.

As Mr. Matherson had been of such importance in the County, it would be a very large affair.

His wife certainly did not look very unhappy, but Jaela thought that she must have had a hard time these last years since he had been crippled.

'She is being more sensible than if she was weeping and wailing,' she told herself as they walked along the passage.

They went down a secondary staircase at the end of the first floor that led them towards the Tower.

Jaela was aware that there were Priests' Holes, secret passages and dungeons in many of the old houses in England and her father had often talked about them.

In their own house in the country there was a secret passage that was always supposed to have been used by a

Compton who was an ardent Royalist and he had hidden there from the Cromwellian troops and thereby saved his life.

As The Castle was much older, she thought that, if Mrs. Matherson was writing a book about it, it should be extremely interesting.

They reached the ground floor and moved into a part of The Castle that was so old that it was seldom used.

The rooms here, which were small and with low ceilings, appeared to be closed up and the corridor ended where the house joined the great Tower.

When they reached it, instead of going through the door and up the twisting staircase to the top as Kathy and Jaela had done some days previously, Mrs. Matherson turned right.

She now led them down a dark and narrow corridor.

The walls had been panelled at a later period and were clearly very old and the carving on the panels was somewhat crude.

They must by now, Jaela thought, have reached almost the back of the Tower when Mrs. Matherson stopped.

On the ground there was a lantern with a candle burning in it.

She lifted it up and then said to Kathy,

"Now I will show you what I have found."

She ran her fingers along one of the panels and, as Kathy gave a cry of delight, the panel swung open.

"I know that your father will be interested in this," Mrs. Matherson declared.

"But I will see it first," Kathy said, stepping forward.

Jaela reached out her hand.

"Be careful, darling," she warned, "there might be steps."

"There are," Mrs. Matherson agreed, "and that is why I have brought a lantern."

She held it up and said to Kathy,

"Go down very carefully and I will light your way."

Jaela intervened.

"I think that might be rather dangerous," she said. "Let me go first and, when I reach the bottom, I will hold the lantern so that Kathy can see where she is placing her feet."

She was remembering as she spoke how worn the steps were up to the top of the Tower and she was afraid that the child might fall and bruise her knees.

Rather reluctantly, as if she thought that she was interfering, Mrs. Matherson gave Jaela the lantern.

"Very well, Miss Compton," she said. "You go first and Kathy can follow you down the steps. There are only half-a-dozen of them and then the corridor goes straight on."

Holding the lantern low so that she could see the steps clearly, Jaela went slowly down until she reached the bottom.

Her feet were now on hard ground and she turned round to hold up the lantern for Kathy, who was waiting impatiently at the top.

"Come down very slowly, darling," she said, "and hold onto my hand."

She put out her left hand as she spoke and then helped Kathy down the steps, which were rather high and, as she had suspected, worn with age.

"Now we are in a cave!" Kathy cried excitedly as she reached the bottom.

She would have gone on, but Jaela did not release her hand.

"We must wait for Mrs. Matherson," she said.

She held the lantern up as she spoke so that Mrs. Matherson could see her way.

To her surprise she realised that, while she had been helping Kathy down the last step which was higher than the others, the door above them had closed.

"Mrs. Matherson!" Jaela called out.

There was no reply and her voice seemed somehow stifled by the darkness around them.

A thought like a streak of lightning seeped through her mind.

"Mrs. Matherson!" she called again.

When there was still no reply, she knew that they were trapped.

"Where has she gone?" Kathy asked. "She was going to show us the secret passage."

"Yes — I know," Jaela replied in a voice that did not sound like her own, "but perhaps we had better — explore it for ourselves."

Then she had another idea.

"I think we must just see why Mrs. Matherson is not coming with us," she said to Kathy. "Perhaps she feels unwell."

As she spoke, she put the lantern into the child's hand saying,

"Hold this, darling, and don't move, otherwise I may trip on the steps."

"I will hold it for you," Kathy nodded.

Jaela climbed up the steps.

When she reached the door, she realised at once that the panel that covered the wooden door was firmly in place. There was no way of opening it.

Jaela could see no catch and no carving where one could be hidden.

She realised, although it seemed incredible, that Mrs. Matherson was disposing of Kathy and herself.

It made her remember that everyone had been very surprised by Mr. Matherson's death because he was such a strong man.

Jaela was perceptive enough to realise what Mrs. Matherson's feelings were for the Earl.

Although she shrank from admitting it, she was certain that the woman had gone mad.

She was 'clearing the decks' so that there would be nothing to prevent the Earl from marrying her now that she was free.

'It cannot be true! I must be imagining it!' Jaela thought frantically.

But, when she pressed her hand against the door, she knew that there was no possible way of opening it from the inside.

Unless she could find a way out of the secret passage both she and Kathy would die.

"What are you doing, Miss Compton?" Kathy asked from below her. "And where is Mrs. Matherson?"

Jaela drew in her breath.

"I think, darling, she is playing a game with us."

"A game?" Kathy asked as Jaela came carefully down the steps.

"What we have to do is to be very clever and find our way out of the secret passage," she said. "Shall we go and explore?"

"It's very dark," Kathy remarked.

"Yes, it is," Jaela agreed.

She was feeling the terror of what was happening sweeping over her until she wanted to scream for help.

But she knew if she did that it would be useless and would only frighten Kathy.

She reckoned now that they were actually under the Tower itself and far from any human beings.

Not only would no one hear them but no one in The Castle would have the slightest idea where they had gone.

'What shall I do? *Oh, God, what shall I do?*' Jaela asked herself over and over again.

Then, as she took Kathy by the hand, she was praying desperately to her father for help.

'Help us – Papa – *help us!*' she pleaded. 'Kathy and I cannot – die in such a – ridiculous fashion.'

As she prayed, she was moving forward very carefully.

Then suddenly on the left side a short passage opened out in front of them.

In it was something that looked like a heap of rags.

They drew a little nearer and, as they did so, Jaela was aware that the main passage had come to an end.

In front was a solid stone wall.

In fact the place where Mrs. Matherson had imprisoned them was not a passage.

It was nothing more than a cave beneath the Tower that might have been used as a cellar or perhaps a prison.

Jaela stared at the wall in front of them and then looked again at the bundle of rags.

Something gleamed in the centre of it.

She knew with a horror that was just like the cold hand of death that she had found Lady Anstey.

Quickly, in case Kathy should see what she had seen, she then turned the child round and walked back the way they had come.

"Can we not go any further?" Kathy enquired.

"No – darling," Jaela replied.

It was an effort to speak.

When she did so again the words seemed to come jerkily from between her lips.

"I-I think it would be – more comfortable to – sit on the – steps," she said. "The ground – might be damp."

"It's not really a very exciting secret passage, is it, Miss Compton?" Kathy asked her.

"No," Jaela replied. "It was much more fun to climb to the top of the Tower."

"Let's do that again soon," Kathy suggested.

They had reached the steps and Jaela sat down on the lowest one and drew Kathy down beside her.

"I am afraid we shall have to – wait until Mrs. Matherson opens the – panel for us."

"We shall have to say that we could not find another way out," Kathy piped up.

"Yes, I know," Jaela replied, "but I expect she knew that when she showed us in here."

"It's a really silly game," Kathy asserted. "I want to climb up the Tower."

"I know you do and we will do that as soon as we get out of here."

"If we shout, perhaps she will open the door now," Kathy suggested.

Jaela put her arm round Kathy and held her close.

"I will tell you a story," she said, "and then perhaps – you can tell me one."

"You first," Kathy smiled.

Jaela had placed the lantern down at her feet and now she picked it up and put it on the top step.

The light revealed a heavy stone ceiling above them.

The air was not putrid and they could breathe easily.

Jaela was certain that there must be hidden places in the walls so that the air from outside could enter freely.

She suspected when the lantern went out, which would be in one or two hours' time, they might even see a faint glow of daylight from outside.

Even so, however much she shouted or screamed, it would be most unlikely that anyone would hear her.

'Help us – Papa! *Help – us!*' Jaela prayed again.

She felt as she held Kathy even closer that if she had to die, the child, who was so young, must live.

It was only an hour later that the candle in the lantern spluttered and went out.

It was then that Kathy began to be really frightened.

"I don't like being here in the dark, Miss Compton," she pleaded. "Please – let us get – out."

"I wish I could do that," Jaela said, "but I am afraid, darling, that Mrs. Matherson has forgotten all about us."

"Forgotten about us?" Kathy cried. "But we cannot stay here for ever – and we will be – hungry!"

"That is true," Jaela said, "and because Mrs. Matherson has forgotten us, we have to pray very very hard that, when your father comes home and realises that we are missing, he will search the whole of The Castle to find us."

Kathy thought this over and then, because she was an intelligent child, she said,

"Mrs. Matherson said that no one knew of this secret passage except for her."

"I expect your father knows of it," Jaela replied.

Even as she spoke, she knew that no one, least of all the Earl, had any idea that this was the way that Mrs. Matherson had murdered Lady Anstey.

Jaela was still suffering from the shock of seeing the skeleton of her face shining in the light from the lantern.

It was half-covered by rags of what had once been a fashionable gown.

Once again Jaela wanted to scream in abject terror.

But all that mattered was that Kathy should not be frightened or upset.

Jaela could not believe that God had forsaken them and they would be left to die in such a horrible manner.

Aloud she said and her voice was surprisingly steady,

"Now we are both going to say special prayers to our Guardian Angels who are looking after us. Somehow they will tell your father where to find us."

"Do you really think my Guardian Angel can hear me right down here in this nasty dark place?" Kathy asked.

"If you close your eyes and pray very hard, your angel and mine will hear us and be near us," Jaela said with conviction.

Kathy put her hands together and Jaela could hear her murmuring a little prayer beneath her breath.

She felt the tears coming into her eyes.

She next sent out a desperate plea from her heart not only to her Guardian Angel but also to the Earl.

Surely he would understand that something terrible had happened to them?

'Save us – *save* – *us*!' she cried to him.

Then, as she prayed fervently, she realised that, if somebody else besides Myrtle Anstey went missing in so mysterious a manner, the gossips would be at work once again.

Now they would be quite certain that the Earl was a murderer.

They would say that he disposed of her and his child's body in the same way that he had disposed of his mistress.

'Save us – *oh, save – us*!' she was praying again.

She strained every nerve in her body so that her prayers should reach him.

Then she knew that she loved him.

*

The Earl rode back to The Castle late in the afternoon, his spaniels running beside him.

His friend, who owned one of the finest spaniel bitches he thought he had ever seen, had been delighted with all three of his dogs.

"I think we should let Belle have the choice," he suggested to the Earl.

The two men watched as the dogs met each other.

Rover the largest and strongest of the Earl's dogs was obviously the favourite.

The Earl took Rufus and Bracken into his friend's house with him.

The two men were talking together inevitably of dogs and horses until his friend's keeper came to say that everything was in order.

As the Earl rose to go home, his host said reassuringly,

"I shall not forget, Halesworth, that I have promised you the pick of the litter."

"I want a really good puppy for my small daughter, Katherine," the Earl replied.

His friend smiled.

"I had heard that she was back with you."

"Yes, she has come home and I am very happy to have her."

"I hope you will bring her over not only to see my dogs but also to meet my small son. My wife has taken him to visit his grandmother at the moment, but next time you come, bring Katherine with you."

"I certainly will," the Earl promised.

He mounted his horse and rode home, but not going too fast for the spaniels.

He was enjoying, as he always did, the verdant countryside.

It had been raining nearly all the afternoon, but now the sun had come out and everything looked fresh and spring-like.

It make him think of Jaela.

He was aware that there was something very young and spring-like about her.

She also had a very astute brain and talked intelligently on many diverse subjects.

He found that everything she said had an originality about it.

It was something that he had never encountered in a woman before.

He had invariably found that women's conversation became banal after a very short time in their company.

When he was not actually making love to them, he would much rather have a man as a companion.

When he left them, however beautiful they might be, he could remember nothing really stimulating that they had ever said to him.

Even the Russian Ambassador's wife, whom he had not thought of for a long time, had a habit of repeating the same stories that she had told him before and she expected him to laugh at the same jokes.

His thoughts then reverted to Jaela.

'How can she be so young and yet so clever?' he asked himself.

He knew that, until he had found the answer to the puzzle that she had set him, he would never be satisfied.

She was a lady, there was no doubt of that.

She was exquisitely dressed in extremely expensive clothes.

Then for what possible reason was she the Governess to a small child?

And just why was she so mysterious about herself?

Unless, of course, she was hiding from someone.

He thought suddenly that she might be hiding from a husband who was cruel to her.

Alternatively a lover whom she had no wish to marry.

Yet he knew that he would bet his last penny that, despite her appearance and despite her brain, Jaela Compton was very young and innocent.

He was too experienced not to be certain that she had never been kissed.

There was a distinct aura of purity about her.

It was something that he had not found in any other woman he had ever associated with.

Granted, he told himself cynically, he had moved in Society in London where purity was a very rare quality.

At the same time he had no solution to the puzzle that was called 'Jaela Compton'.

'She is certainly unique,' he told himself as The Castle came in sight.

He thought as he rode up to the front door that he would tell Kathy to join him for tea and Jaela Compton would come with her.

He wondered if he dared ask her to dine with him tonight as he would be alone.

Then he thought that it would be a mistake.

The servants would talk and after all she was only a Governess –

He decided therefore that he would send for her after dinner and then he would tell her to bring her father's stamp albums with her.

That at least would be an excuse for them to start a conversation.

When they had exhausted that subject, he would try once again to discover more about her.

A groom was waiting outside The Castle door to take his horse from him.

As he dismounted, he patted Jupiter on the neck.

"He is in good trim," he said to the groom.

The man grinned.

"Aye, my Lord, and you can say that about all your Lordship's 'orses!"

"That is what I would expect," the Earl replied.

He walked up the steps and into the hall.

Whitlock was waiting for him with two footmen in attendance.

One of them took the Earl's hat and another his gloves.

"I will have tea in the study," he said to Whitlock.

"It's all ready and waitin' for your Lordship," Whitlock replied.

"Ask her Ladyship and Miss Compton to join me," the Earl said as he walked towards the study.

Two of his spaniels followed him, but Rufus ran up the stairs beside the footman to the nursery.

The footman had found that the nursery was empty.

He then looked into both the bedrooms before he came downstairs again.

He told Whitlock that they were not there.

Whitlock went into the study and the Earl looked up when he entered.

"There's no sign of her Ladyship in the nursery, my Lord," Whitlock said, "but they've not to my knowledge gone out and Charles has been in the hall all the afternoon."

"Then they must be somewhere in The Castle," the Earl ordered. "Find them!"

"Very good, my Lord."

Some time later the Earl poured himself a cup of tea and there was still no news from Whitlock.

There was now a worried expression in his eyes.

He wondered what Jaela Compton could be doing with the child.

He thought that she might have anticipated that he would want to see Kathy as soon as he returned home.

Whitlock came into the study.

"We have searched and made enquiries in the stables, my Lord," he reported, "but they have not been there since this morning."

"Have you looked everywhere in The Castle?" the Earl asked.

"Everywhere, my Lord."

"And nobody has seen them since luncheon?"

"No, my Lord."

Whitlock hesitated.

"What is it?" the Earl enquired.

"Well, my Lord, one of the stable lads, when I questioned him, thought he sees a horse bein' ridden away from the Tower early this afternoon."

"Who was riding it?" the Earl asked sharply.

"The lad said 'twere a woman, my Lord, and he thought, although he was not too certain' 'twere Mrs. Matherson."

The Earl stared at him.

"Mrs. Matherson?" he repeated incredulously. "I think that extremely unlikely."

"I thought the same, my Lord," Whitlock agreed, "seein' as how the funeral has not yet taken place."

"And the horse was coming from the Tower?"

"That's what the lad says, my Lord."

The Earl was thinking of how Sybil Matherson had come to him at night.

She slipped through a door beside the Tower that no one else ever used.

He rose to his feet and the three spaniels, who had flopped down on the hearthrug, sat up expectantly.

Rufus, who had come downstairs with the footman from the nursery, had come into the study with Whitlock.

The Earl walked out of the study and along the passage that led towards the Tower.

And all the dogs followed him.

He was wondering furiously what Sybil, if it had in fact been Sybil, was doing in The Castle.

Why she should come there in his absence?

She could hardly be visiting his bedroom early in the afternoon.

Yet if it had been just an ordinary call to ask his help in planning the funeral, why had she not come to the front door?

It was then he had a premonition that something was very wrong.

He knew, as he thought about it, that it was something he had felt already while riding home.

It was nothing that he could put into words and yet the feeling had been there all the time he had been thinking of Jaela.

Now he was becoming really apprehensive.

He then reached the end of The Castle and entered the old part of the building where the rooms had been shut up for a long time.

At the far end was the Tower.

Beside it on the left side was the door that Sybil used when she visited him and he knew that it led out into the garden.

He then opened the other door, which led into the Tower itself.

Now, as if he felt that he had to hurry, he ran up the twisting steps very quickly.

The door to the roof was closed and, even as he opened it, he knew that it was unlikely that he would find them outside.

One glance told him that there was no one there and the roof itself was still wet from the rain earlier in the afternoon.

He turned and went back down the steps.

Now he was desperately afraid of what might have happened to Kathy and Jaela.

'Where the devil can they be?' he asked himself again and again.

As the spaniels followed him out through the door, he closed it.

He started walking back the way he had come.

He wondered desperately where he should search next and the memory swept over him that this was what he had done before.

It was when he had searched for Myrtle and had failed completely to find her.

"Oh, my God!" he swore beneath his breath. "This cannot be happening again."

Only when he had moved past the first closed room was he aware of a strange sound behind him.

He looked back.

Two of the dogs were at his heels, but Rufus was missing.

It was then that he heard the same sound that had alerted him a moment before.

He walked back and realised that it came from the passage that curved round the Tower.

He knew a little further on it came to an abrupt end and it had been closed and bricked up a century earlier.

He whistled, but he could still hear a continuous scratching noise.

He walked on and then he saw to his astonishment Rufus scratching wildly at the oak panelling that covered part of the passage.

The Earl reached him.

"What are you doing, old boy?" he asked. "You cannot go through a wooden wall."

Rufus paid no attention.

He was still busy scratching and whining and then scratching again frantically with both his front paws.

It was then that the Earl stared at the panelling.

He remembered that there were other passages in the house that could be entered only by a secret catch.

It was usually concealed in the carved wood.

While he was thinking, Rufus was still scratching away.

The Earl ran his fingers along the panelling above the spaniel's head.

It took him only a few seconds to find it.

Then, as he pressed something that was embedded in the wood, the panel opened.

Before the Earl could pull the panel wide enough for himself, Rufus had sprung through the aperture.

The dog threw himself down the steps.

There was a cry of delight, which came from Kathy.

Then she was struggling and stumbling up the steps to her father.

"Papa! *Papa!*" she cried. "I have been – praying for you to come and – save me! I was – afraid. Oh – Papa, I was so – frightened in that nasty – dark – place."

The Earl lifted her up in his arms and she hid her tear-stained face against his shoulder.

"It is all right, my darling," he said in a soothing voice.

Then, as he realised that she was crying, he saw Jaela come slowly up the steps towards him.

She was very pale but, while there were tears in her eyes, she was smiling.

The Earl put out his hand and she clasped it with both of hers.

"You are all right?" he asked.

He felt her fingers trembling.

"I-It has been – very frightening," she said in a voice that he could hardly hear, "but – Kathy was – very b-brave."

"We have been – here for hours and – hours in the – dark," Kathy complained.

"It was Rufus who found you," the Earl told her, "and you must thank him."

"Rufus – *oh* – *Rufus*!" Kathy cried.

She looked down at the dog who was jumping up against the Earl's legs.

He put her down on the ground.

Kathy flung her arms around Rufus and hid her face in his soft fur.

The Earl looked at Jaela.

"What happened?" he asked her.

"It – it was Mrs. Matherson," she answered, "and – and I have – something to – tell you, but – not in front of – Kathy."

The Earl's fingers tightened on hers.

She thought that it was the most comforting feeling that she had ever had.

Then, as she looked into his eyes, she felt that they were speaking to each other without words.

He realised just how desperate she had been.

She felt that he must have been aware of how she had prayed for him to come and save them.

"There is tea waiting for you, Kathy, in the study," the Earl said to his daughter, "and I think Rufus deserves a large piece of cake."

"That is what I will give him!" Kathy replied. "Oh, clever, clever Rufus, to find us!"

She hugged the spaniel again.

Then she rose to her feet to run down the passage with the dog following her.

The Earl relinquished Jaela's hand and they walked after Kathy.

"Are you saying," he asked in a low voice, "that Sybil Matherson intended to kill you?"

Jaela drew in her breath.

"Lady – Anstey is – in there," she related. "I s-saw her – skeleton – although Kathy was not – aware of it!"

The Earl stiffened as he stipulated,

"I had no idea that this place existed!"

"Mrs. Matherson came to the nursery to tell – us that she had just – discovered it. And I think she meant to – kill Kathy there – alone, but I insisted – on going too."

"Thank God for that!" the Earl expostulated.

They walked on and joined Kathy in the study.

Only as they did so was Jaela aware that tears of relief were running down her cheeks.

She would have gone upstairs to her room in the nursery.

But the Earl sat her down very gently in an armchair and gave her his handkerchief.

"There is no hurry," he said quietly. "I have found you and I am thanking God on my knees that neither of you are hurt."

Jaela looked up at him with her tear-filled eyes and he knew that he loved her as he had never loved a woman before.

She was his and he would never lose her again.

CHAPTER SEVEN

The Earl went to the tea table and poured out a cup of tea.

He then took it to the grog tray and added a little brandy before he handed the cup over to Jaela.

She felt almost too weak to take it from him.

"Drink it," he insisted quietly.

She took a sip and, realising that there was brandy in it, made a little grimace.

"All of it," the Earl ordered her.

Because it was easier to obey him than to argue, Jaela did as she was told.

Then the Earl put the cup and saucer down on the table and said to Kathy,

"Come here, Kathy, I want to talk to you."

"I have given Rufus a large piece of cake," Kathy said, "but Bracken and Rover looked jealous, so I have given them some too."

"I want you to listen to me," the Earl said.

She rose from her chair obediently and went to his side.

He lifted her onto his knee.

"Now listen to what I have to say," he said quietly. "You and Miss Compton have had a very nasty experience."

"I was very – very – frightened in that – dark place," Kathy answered.

"I know you were, my poppet," the Earl replied.

"What is a poppet?" Kathy asked.

"A very brave girl who is very clever," the Earl smiled.

"Is that me?"

"That is you, And I want you to promise me, and that includes Miss Compton, that what happened is a secret."

"A secret?" Kathy questioned.

"A secret that only you, Miss Compton, I and Rufus know."

Kathy gave a little laugh.

"Rufus will not talk."

"And nor must you," the Earl warned her.

"Why?" Kathy enquired.

"Because it was a stupid trick played on you by a bad woman and I don't want anybody to know that you were so foolish as to do as she suggested."

"She is very very bad!" Kathy persevered indignantly.

"I agree with you," the Earl said, "but I want you to promise me on your honour that neither you nor Miss Compton will talk about it to anybody in The Castle and outside as well."

He looked at Jaela as he spoke and she vowed,

"I-I promise."

"I promise too," Kathy said. "Now can I give Rufus some more cake?"

"I think he deserves it," the Earl answered.

Impulsively Kathy put her arms round her father's neck.

"Thank you, Papa, as well as Rufus for saving us from that horrible woman."

Before he could speak, she jumped down off his knee and Jaela saw the expression in his eyes.

She knew that what she had hoped had come true. The Earl loved his little daughter as much as she did. He rose to his feet and, going towards Jaela, he put out his hand to help her out of the chair.

"You are to go up to bed," he said. "You have been through enough for today."

She did not reply, but almost instinctively her fingers clung to his.

"I will explain that you have a headache," he went on, "and I will bring Kathy up later and Elsie can put her to bed."

Jaela made a little murmur, but she did not protest as he led her towards the door.

Then, as he opened it for her, he raised her hand to his lips and kissed it.

"Thank you," he said to her quietly.

She walked out of the study and he closed the door behind her.

When Jaela reached her bedroom, she knew that she was exhausted to the point where she still felt faint.

It was an almost superhuman effort to undress.

In bed she knew that the Earl was right, she had been through enough.

She thought that she would never forget the agony that she had felt in the darkness and only by continually talking to Kathy and telling her stories could she prevent the child from becoming hysterical.

She had kept wondering how long it would take for them to die.

But she hoped and prayed that Kathy would die first so that the child would not be alone.

Now it was all over.

The Earl had saved them.

'He is – *wonderful*,' she whispered to herself. 'And I – love him!'

Then she fell into a deep exhausted sleep.

*

The following morning the Earl did not go riding as usual, but instead he came down to breakfast rather late.

Before he left his bedroom he had sent a groom with one of his fastest horses to ask the Chief Constable to call on him as soon as it was possible.

He was thinking all the time he was waiting for him what exactly he should say to him about the finding of Lady Anstey's body.

It was only when he had finished breakfast that he realised that he had not read a word of the newspaper that was propped up in front of him.

He picked it up and carried it into the study.

Ignoring the pile of letters that had been placed on his desk, he sat down in an armchair and opened *The Morning Post*.

His brain however refused to assimilate a report on the political situation, nor the return of the Prince of Wales from the Marienbad Spar.

Instead he was debating with himself whether or not he should involve Sybil Matherson in what had occurred.

He thought if he told even the Chief Constable the truth, it might well result in a torrid scandal.

He was still turning the problem over in his mind when the door then opened and without being announced Sybil Matherson walked in.

For a moment he did not move, but merely stared at her incredulously.

She closed the door and ran across the room towards him.

"Dearest Stafford," she began, "I had to come and see you. I have just heard that your daughter is missing and I know how worried and anxious you must be."

She looked at him yearningly.

With an effort the Earl rose to his feet.

"Do you know what you are saying, Sybil?" he asked.

"I heard this morning when I woke up that dear little Katherine is missing. Oh, Stafford, I am so, so sorry. I had to be at your side to help and comfort you in your distress."

The Earl continued to stare at her, but he did not speak.

Then he was aware that her hands were on his shoulders and her lips were raised to his.

"One moment, Sybil," he retorted.

Putting her on one side, he walked across the room and opened the door.

There was no sign of any servant.

He realised that Sybil must have come to him secretly through the door in the Tower.

It took him only a few moments to reach the hall and to say to the footman who was on duty there,

"Ask Miss Compton to come to the study immediately."

"Very good, my Lord."

The Earl went back into the study.

"Where have you been?" Sybil Matherson asked him suspiciously.

"Making certain that we are not disturbed," the Earl replied.

Her face lit up and she purred,

"Oh, dearest wonderful Stafford, it is hard to tell you how much I miss you, but after the funeral tomorrow, when Edward's tiresome relations have left, we can be together.'

"Is that what you want?" the Earl asked her.

"You know I want it," Sybil Matherson said. "I love you. Oh, Stafford, I love you."

There was a note in her voice that the Earl thought had a touch of hysteria in it.

He walked away from her to stand with his back to the fireplace.

"Tell me how you are aware that Katherine is missing?" he asked.

"It is what I was told," Sybil Matherson said. "I cannot imagine what has happened."

The Earl did not reply and she said after a moment,

"Perhaps she has tried to go back to Italy to look for her mother. Children find it difficult to adjust themselves to a new place."

The Earl's lips tightened.

There was an expression in his eyes that anyone else would have known was ominous.

Then the door opened and he looked round expectantly.

But it was Whitlock who entered to announce,

"The Chief Constable, Sir Alexander Langton, my Lord."

The Chief Constable, a distinguished-looking man who had commanded the Coldstream Guards, came into the room.

He was wearing driving clothes and the Earl knew that he must have left immediately he received his message.

The Earl walked towards him and held out his hand.

"It was kind of you to come, Sir Alexander," he said, "as I need you urgently."

The Chief Constable looked surprised and the Earl went on,

"I think you know Mrs. Matherson?"

"Yes, of course," the Chief Constable replied.

He shook her hand.

"My deepest condolences," he said, "I was, as you know, very fond of your husband and we shall all miss him."

Mrs. Matherson was just about to reply when Jaela came into the room.

Watching Sybil Matherson's face, the Earl was aware that she froze into immobility.

She stared at Jaela as if she was seeing a ghost rather than a human being.

Whitlock closed the door and the Earl said,

"Good morning, Miss Compton. I think you know Mrs. Matherson? And may I introduce Sir Alexander Langton, the Chief Constable of the County."

Jaela dropped a small curtsey first to Mrs. Matherson and next to the Chief Constable.

Then the Earl, without asking anyone to sit down, began,

"I have asked you here, Chief Constable, because I want Miss Compton to tell you how she found yesterday afternoon the remains of Lady Anstey, who you will remember has been missing for so long."

He paused for a moment before he added,

"And, as Mrs. Matherson is now here, she can explain just why after she had discovered Lady Anstey's skeleton, she did not inform anyone where it was."

There was a tense silence.

The Chief Constable looked first at Jaela and then at Mrs. Matherson.

The Earl was also watching her carefully and then she started and the words seemed to tumble from her lips.

"I am sure, Chief Constable, you will not listen to any nonsense that is related to you by a mere servant! And if you are insinuating, Stafford, that I had anything at all to do with the disappearance of Myrtle Anstey, it is a lie, do you hear me? A lie!"

Her voice rose to a shriek and Jaela said quietly,

"It was you, Mrs. Matherson, who locked Lady Katherine and me in that ghastly dark cavern under the Tower! And after you left us to die, as you had obviously left Lady Anstey, I saw her bones."

She spoke quietly and calmly and Mrs. Matherson threw up her hands.

"You are lying, lying, *lying*!" she shouted. "I was not even in The Castle yesterday and you cannot prove that I was."

She turned to the Chief Constable, saying,

"This woman here, who calls herself a Governess, has been trying to curry favour with his Lordship! Don't you listen to her. Is it likely that I would murder Lady Anstey or anybody else?"

"It certainly seems incredible, Mrs. Matherson," the Chief Constable replied, "but in my position I am obliged to listen to everything that Miss Compton has to say."

"Miss Compton! Miss Compton!" Mrs. Matherson then exclaimed, seeming to spit out the name. "Why should you listen to her?"

The Chief Constable turned to Jaela, drawing a notebook from his pocket as he did so.

Then he looked at the Earl who said

"Do sit down at my desk, Sir Alexander. It will be more comfortable for you."

The Chief Constable moved as the Earl spoke and, putting his notebook down on the top of the blotter, he then took a pencil from the Earl's pen tray.

As he did so, Sybil Matherson put her hand on the Earl's arm.

"There is no reason for me to stay and listen to this tissue of lies, Stafford."

"As you are here," the Earl responded coldly, "you must stay!"

The Chief Constable was looking at Jaela, who was standing to the left of the desk.

"Perhaps we should start, Miss Compton," he said in a businesslike tone, "by your giving me your full name."

"It is 'Jaela Compton' and I am the daughter of Lord Compton of Mellor, who was before his retirement the Lord High Chancellor of England."

The Earl gave a start and the Chief Constable said,

"I knew your father, Miss Compton, and admired him enormously. I had no idea that I would meet his daughter here at The Castle."

There was a note of surprise in his voice, which Jaela recognised and so did the Earl.

"I must explain," he said quickly, "that Miss Compton has only just returned to England and we are to be married very shortly."

The Chief Constable smiled.

He was about to speak when there was a shrill shriek from Mrs. Matherson.

"Marry her? You are not going to marry her, Stafford. You are going to marry *me*! I love you, you know I love you!"

She tried to throw herself against him, but the Earl put out his arm and held her away from him.

"Control yourself, Sybil," he demanded sharply.

"You are going to marry *me*!" she shouted. "I killed Edward so that you could do so. I killed that Anstey woman and I killed your daughter! There is now no one to stop you from being mine do you hear? Mine – *mine*!"

There was silence as the Earl, the Chief Constable and Jaela stared at her.

Even in her madness, Mrs. Matherson realised what she had said.

Shouting, "you are mine! *You are mine*, she rushed towards the door.

They could hear her voice shouting *"Mine, mine, mine."* as she ran into the hall.

Those left behind seemed to be frozen into immobility.

Then, as if the Earl realised that he must go and see what was happening, he strode from the room.

Crossing the hall, he reached the top of the steps outside the front door.

He saw Mrs. Matherson driving away in a chaise drawn by two fine horses.

It belonged not to her but to the Chief Constable.

She had jumped into the driving seat, picked up the reins and slashed at the horses with a whip.

The groom had been talking to one of the footmen at the bottom of the steps and now he had run a little way after her only to stop and stare at the departing chaise.

A few seconds later it disappeared under the oak trees that bordered the drive.

"That's the Chief Constable's chaise, my Lord," Whitlock said unnecessarily to the Earl.

He did not reply, but walked back into the study.

"I am so sorry to tell you, Sir Alexander," he said, "that Mrs. Matherson has taken your chaise and horses."

The Chief Constable sighed.

"She is obviously mad! However, the disappearance of Lady Anstey, which has always troubled me, has now been solved."

He looked at the Earl as he spoke.

They were both aware that he was free at last of the stigma that unless this had happened it would have followed him to his grave.

The Chief Constable rose to his feet.

"I am afraid, Halesworth, I shall have to rely on you to convey me home. I must also try to see on the way what has happened to my horses."

"I am sure that Whitlock will already have sent a message to the stables," the Earl said, "so let me offer you some refreshment before you leave."

The Chief Constable shook his head.

"I have only just had breakfast," he said, "and I consider it important that I should get in touch immediately with Mrs. Matherson."

The Earl did not argue and the Chief Constable held out his hand to Jaela.

"I feel sure we shall meet again soon, Miss Compton," he said, "and let me tell you that your father will always be remembered for his brilliance and his wit. We in this country are very much the poorer with his passing."

"Thank you," Jaela said softly. "I miss him unbearably, as you will understand. At the same time he is no longer suffering."

The Chief Constable put his hand on her shoulder.

"That is a brave girl," he said. "And you have a very clever young man to look after you. I hope you will invite me to your Wedding."

He did not wait for a reply, but walked from the room and the Earl followed him.

Jaela moved to the window and looked out at the sunlit garden.

She could hardly believe what had just happened or that the Earl, in order to save her reputation, had said that they were to be married.

She had always known it would shock people if they learnt that, as her father's daughter, she was staying alone in The Castle without a chaperone.

Especially with someone as handsome as the Earl.

Now she decided that she must make it easy for him to keep his freedom and she knew before he came back what she must say.

She was still looking out of the window and the sun turned her hair to a halo of gold.

Very slowly the Earl walked across the room to stand behind her.

As he drew closer, she felt herself trembling. Her heart was behaving in a very strange manner.

"Why did you not tell me who you were?" he asked. "And I am exceedingly thankful that nobody will continue to think that I might be a murderer."

"You – knew they – thought that?" she asked.

"I am not a fool," the Earl replied, "and I saw it in their eyes, heard it in the tone of their voices and when they stopped speaking when I came into a room."

"It must have been horrible for you!"

"It has been a nightmare, which I hope now I shall be able to forget."

She did not speak and, after a moment or two, he said,

"If I had lost you and Kathy, I think I would have taken my own life!"

"Instead – we are both safe," Jaela said quickly, "and I have been – thinking while you were – out of the room how you could – rid yourself of me."

"Do you think that is what I want!" the Earl asked.

"You have saved my reputation," Jaela said, "and now I must – save your – freedom."

"How do you propose to do that?"

"I think the best thing would be, as soon as you find someone else to look after Kathy – for me to go back to Italy."

She drew in her breath before she went on,

"After two or perhaps three months – when I do not return, you can announce – that we have changed our minds and there is no longer any question of our being – married."

"And that is what you want to happen?" the Earl enquired.

She longed so much to tell him how much she wanted to stay with him and Kathy.

But she knew that it was impossible now that she had revealed who she was so that the Chief Constable would believe what she had said about Mrs. Matherson.

Perhaps, she thought, he might have believed her anyway.

All she had done therefore was to precipitate the Earl into announcing their engagement in order to save her reputation.

Because she loved him she felt that she could not tie him to her when he had no wish to be tied.

She then carried on quickly,

"If, in a week or so's time, I disappear to Italy, I shall soon be forgotten – only please – please – find someone who will love Kathy. She is such an adorable child and I could not bear her to think of her being unhappy."

"I think it would be extremely difficult, if not impossible, to find someone who loves her as much as you do," the Earl remarked.

Jaela made a helpless little gesture with her hands before she said,

"There must be someone – kind who will teach her all the things she needs to know."

"I doubt if they would be as efficient as you are," the Earl responded softly.

"But – we have to find – someone!" Jaela asserted desperately.

"Are you so keen to leave me that you are prepared to make Kathy unhappy as well as me?"

"You?" Jaela asked.

She was so surprised that without meaning to she turned round to look at him.

There was an expression in his eyes that held her spellbound.

She just stared at him.

"For the first time since I have known you," the Earl said, "you are being foolish and extremely stupid."

"B-but – why?" Jaela asked.

"I think I can explain it to you a little more easily this way."

He took a step nearer to her and put his arms around her.

Then, as she looked up at him in astonishment, his lips came down on hers.

For a moment she could hardly believe what was happening.

Then, as she felt his mouth hold her captive, her whole being seemed to come alive.

Instinctively she moved closer and still closer to him.

As he kissed her, she felt as if the sunshine from outside had flooded into the room and shafts of it were running through her body.

The Earl's kisses were very possessive.

And she knew that he was telling her without words that she could not escape from him.

It was so wonderful, and at the same time so incredible, that she felt the tears come into her eyes from the sheer rapture of it.

The sensations he gave her were unlike anything that she had ever known before.

The Earl raised his head.

In a strange little voice that was very unlike her own, she whispered,

"I – love – you, I love – you!"

"As I love you!" he answered. "And I will never lose you."

Then he was kissing her again.

Kissing her until it was no longer possible to think but only to feel that she was a part of the sunshine itself.

There was no longer any fear or unhappiness but only love.

*

A long time later Jaela found herself sitting on a large sofa with her head on the Earl's shoulder and his arms around her.

"How can you be so beautiful," he asked, "and at the same time so clever?"

"How could I have guessed that you – loved me?" Jaela then asked him.

"I have been fighting against my love ever since the first moment I saw you," he related.

"But – you tried to – send Kathy and me – away!" Jaela replied,

"I was saying one thing and thinking another," the Earl answered. "When I saw you the next day, I felt something very strange happen to my heart, but I was completely determined not to acknowledge that it was *love*."

"I was – trying to hate you – after all the wicked things that were said about you."

The Earl laughed.

"I think we are both much too enquiring and too perceptive to be deceived for long."

He paused.

Then he quizzed her in a more serious tone,

"Did you really believe that I had murdered the missing woman?"

"No," Jaela replied truthfully. "You might be overbearing and autocratic, but I just knew that it was impossible for you to do anything so underhand and to be, for want of a better word, ungentlemanly."

The Earl laughed again.

Then he asked her,

"And now? What do you think of me now?"

"You know the answer to that without my putting it into words," Jaela said. "I love you – I love you as I never thought it – possible to love anyone."

"Will you be happy to live here at The Castle with Kathy and me?" the Earl asked.

"I would be happy anywhere with you," Jaela answered, "and I adore The Castle. At the same time, because you are so clever, I think there will be things for you to do in London, and perhaps when we travel together looking for stamps to add to our collection, there will be special missions for you to undertake abroad."

She looked up at him from under her eyelashes as she spoke.

The Earl's arms further tightened round her.

"How can you be so exactly what I have always wanted as my wife?" he asked her. "Of course, my precious, we will do all those things and I know exactly why you are saying that to me."

He kissed her forehead before he went on,

"When we have finished honeymooning, and it is going to take a long time, we will take Kathy with us on many of our trips, as I realise now that your father took you, and maybe some of our children."

Jaela gave a little choked laugh and whispered,

"*Some* – of our children?"

"The nursery is very big."

"That is – what I thought."

He drew her closer still before he said,

"My darling, I know from the way that you look after and protect Kathy that you love children. I want a son and several brothers and sisters for him and Kathy, so that none of them will ever be lonely as I have been these past years until I met you."

"You were an only child as I was," Jaela said, "but, darling, I will make sure that your large and beautiful nursery is filled with our babies – as long as you don't stop – loving me."

She looked up at him.

Although she was teasing him, there was a serious note in her voice as she added,

"I could not accept these tiresome women who fall so hysterically in love with you trying to interfere. It will not be you who will murder them but me!"

"Do you really think I could find anyone who could excite me more than you?" the Earl asked. "It is not only by your lips and your exquisite body but also by your brilliant brain."

He kissed her forehead again before he added,

"There is an intriguing enchantment in everything you say. I have gone to bed at night thinking and puzzling over you, until I began to think that you were an enigma that I would never understand or a maze of which I would never reach the centre."

"Now you know," Jaela said quietly, "that the centre of it is my heart – and you fill it completely. And, darling, I only hope you will not be – bored now that I am no longer an enigma, a maze or a puzzle."

"I will answer that question in fifty years' time," the Earl grinned.

Then he was kissing her again.

Kissing her until she thought that no one could be so happy and not be in Heaven.

They went upstairs to the nursery.

Kathy was being looked after by Elsie and, as they went into the room, she then jumped up and ran towards her father.

"Where have you been, Papa?" she asked. "Miss Compton went away and I wanted to come downstairs, but Elsie would not let me."

"You can come down now," the Earl replied, "but first there is something I want to tell you."

Elsie tactfully left the room and he picked his daughter up and sat her on his knee.

"I want to ask you," he said, "if you like living at The Castle."

"Of course I do," Kathy said. "It is very big and exciting and I was so happy until I was shut up in that horrid dark cave!"

"I am having it bricked up so that no one will ever be locked in it again," the Earl told her

"That will be a good thing," Kathy said. "I was very very frightened."

"Now I have another question to ask you," the Earl went on. "Who do you love in The Castle?"

Kathy laughed and held up her hand.

"I love Rufus," she said turning down one finger, "I love Miss Compton and I love you, Papa."

She hesitated and then added,

"That is three, is it not, Miss Compton?"

"Yes, that is three," Jaela replied.

"I love Miss Compton too," the Earl said, "and I think, Kathy, you and I would be very upset if she left us."

Kathy looked at Jaela.

"Left us?" she asked. "Why should she leave us? I want Miss Compton – to stay."

"So do I," the Earl agreed, "so I am going to make sure that she cannot go away."

"How are you going to do that?" Kathy asked.

"There is really only one safe way to stop her ever escaping," the Earl said, "and that is if she marries me and becomes my wife."

Kathy was obviously surprised and considered this idea for a moment.

She put her head on one side before she answered,

"You are my Papa, so if you marry Miss Compton, then she will be my Mama."

"She will," the Earl agreed, "and what I would like her to do is to give you a brother or a sister to play with."

Jaela held her breath.

She knew that the Earl was being very clever in the way he was telling Kathy what they had planned.

She could only pray that it would all be successful.

There was what seemed to her to be a long pause and then Kathy said,

"I would love to have a brother or a sister and Miss Compton to be my Mama."

"That is what I hoped you would feel," the Earl smiled.

"And, if you are – really going to marry her," Kathy added, "then please – may I be a bridesmaid? I have always wanted to be one, but nobody has ever asked me."

"You shall be my only and most important bridesmaid," Jaela promised.

She looked at the Earl and he saw that her eyes were full of tears.

They were tears of happiness.

Kathy jumped off her father's knee to tell Rufus that she was going to be a bridesmaid.

The Earl said gently to Jaela,

"Everything is just as I wanted it to be, my darling one, and now all we have to do is get married."

*

After luncheon was finished, because the Earl thought that it would take their minds off everything that had happened, he took Jaela and Kathy riding with him.

They rode slowly across the Park.

When they reached the flat ground where they could gallop, the Earl sent Kathy ahead of him.

He told her to wait at the far end and they would race their horses up to her and she could then tell them who was the winner.

"Ride very carefully, dearest," Jaela said. "There is no hurry."

"I am quite safe," Kathy replied. "Snowball is very very careful with me."

She rode away.

After watching her, Jaela turned her head to find that the Earl was looking at her.

"She is so — adorable," she said impulsively.

"The same word applies to you too," he added. "I love you! I love you and I want to go on saying it all the time!"

Jaela drew in her breath.

She thought as she looked up into his eyes that she and Kathy might at this moment have been in the dark cavern.

Without food or water and growing weaker every minute they would not have been alive for long.

Then, as she knew that the Earl was waiting, she said,

"All I — want to do — is to make you and Kathy — happy."

They rode home.

When they reached the house an hour later, there was an expression on Whitlock's face which told the Earl that he wanted to speak to him alone.

While Jaela took Kathy upstairs, he went into the study and Whitlock followed him.

"What is it?" the Earl asked him.

"I thinks your Lordship ought to know," Whitlock replied, "that when Mrs. Matherson took off in the Chief Constable's chaise, she drove so fast out of the gates that she collided with a farm wagon."

"Collided?" the Earl exclaimed.

"The horses was out of hand, my Lord, the chaise turned over and Mrs. Matherson were thrown out of it."

"Is she badly injured?" the Earl enquired.

"She were kicked and trampled on by the horses as her lay on the ground, my Lord, and she died afore the Chief Constable came to the scene of the accident."

The Earl was silent.

He knew at once that it was the best thing that could have happened.

Now the Chief Constable need take no further action against a woman who had admitted to him in front of witnesses that she had killed her husband.

Besides which she was responsible for the gruesome death of Lady Anstey.

He knew that just as Jaela's prayers to him when she and Kathy were shut up in the cave had been heard, so had his that there would be no scandal.

Aloud he said,

"Have they removed Lady Anstey's remains, Whitlock, and taken them, as I ordered, to the Church?"

"The men took the coffin there immediate after luncheon, my Lord," Whitlock replied. "It travelled, as you'd arranged, in the brake, and the Vicar were waitin' to receive it."

"Thank you, Whitlock."

He had left him in charge of the whole operation having decided last night that he would bury Myrtle Anstey at once.

Then he would inform her relatives later what had happened.

He was certain that none of them would want the newspapers to be interested in what had occurred.

What mattered was that she was buried in consecrated ground.

He thought now that at last everything was clear for his marriage.

Just as Whitlock was leaving the room he said,

"Send a message to the Vicar that I would like to see him this evening, say at about six o'clock."

"Very good, my Lord," Whitlock answered.

*

No one was more excited at the thought of the Wedding than Kathy.

She was, however, told to keep it a secret until the evening of the following day.

"You can tell Rufus, but no one else," Jaela said to her.

"But I *am* to be a bridesmaid?"

"Of course you are, dearest, and shall we choose your prettiest dress to wear? Then we can arrange for you to have a wreath of real flowers on your head and you will then carry a bouquet of them."

Kathy was so thrilled that Jaela hardly had time to plan what she herself should wear.

She wanted to look lovely for the Earl and was well aware of just how many beautiful women there had been in his life.

She hesitated over her gowns and she was only grateful that she had so many.

Included amongst those that she had brought to The Castle was one which had been very expensive.

Yet it was so pretty that she had been unable to resist it.

It was white, which was so traditional for brides and was of chiffon, which revealed the curves of her figure and her tiny waist.

It flounced out in frill upon frill that made a long train behind her.

It was an evening gown and the neckline was embroidered with tiny diamanté. It looked so like the dew on the flowers first thing in the morning.

When Jaela put it on, it was so soft and clinging that it made her look ethereal.

It was an ideal perfect frame for the fine lace veil that had been in the Earl's family for generations and which might have been made by Fairy fingers.

The Earl refused to allow her to wear a tiara.

"There will be several available," he said, "when you take your place as a Peeress at the Opening of Parliament."

Instead both she and Kathy wore wreaths of white orchids from the greenhouses.

They had just come into bloom and they carried bouquets of the same flowers.

"This is the first time that they have bloomed since I brought them from abroad," the Earl said. "I think they must have known that they would be wanted for a special occasion."

"A very – very – special occasion," Jaela whispered.

She went downstairs with a very excited Kathy following her.

She thought when she reached the hall that no one could look more handsome or more impressive than the Earl.

He was wearing full evening dress and all his decorations.

When Jaela reached him and looked up at him through her veil, he knew that she was the pure and innocent wife who he had always wanted.

But she was also the cleverest and most intelligent woman he had ever known.

'I am so lucky', he told himself as Jaela took his arm.

He led her down the corridor in the opposite direction to the Tower to the Private Chapel.

It had been added to the house towards the end of the eighteenth century and had been designed by Robert Adam himself.

It was a lovely Chapel and the Vicar carne every month to conduct a special Service for those employed in the house and on the estate.

Now there was no one in the Chapel but the Vicar with Whitlock and Mrs. Hudson.

They had been let into the secret of their marriage so that they could be witnesses at the Service.

The whole Chapel was massed with banks of flowers.

Those on the Altar were white.

But many of the rest came from the gardens and were the bright gold of the daffodils and kingcups.

On the sills below the stained-glass windows there were masses of primroses and violets.

It was very springlike and the Earl thought as he moved slowly up the aisle that it was for him the spring of a new life.

A life that would be very different from what he had endured in the last eight years.

To Jaela it was a Service of the sanctity of love.

She was sure that her father and mother were present and giving them their support and love.

'Thank you, Papa – thank you, Mama,' she prayed as they knelt before the Altar. 'I shall be as happy as you were and in the future I know that not only my husband but you also will both look after me.'

They knelt for the Blessing from the Vicar.

As she did so, she knew that the Guardian Angels who had preserved her and Kathy were also in the Chapel and were singing songs of love.

*

A wildly excited Kathy joined them for dinner with them and drank their health with a small sip of champagne.

When she had been sent to bed, Jaela and her husband were at last alone.

"Everything has been arranged for our honeymoon, my precious," the Earl told her.

"They will come?"

"I have received a note from Elizabeth saying that she and Cousin Henry will stay at The Castle for as long as we are away."

"I am so glad," Jaela cried.

"Also," the Earl went on, "they will bring their young granddaughter with them who is the same age as Kathy."

"Now I can think only of you," Jaela whispered softly.

They went slowly up the stairs hand-in-hand.

Jaela had moved into the beautiful State room where all the Countesses of Halesworth had slept for generations.

Having undressed, Jaela climbed into the huge bed with its carved and gilded posts.

Overhead there was a canopy on which Cupids and doves were joined by garlands of roses.

Jaela waited.

Then the communicating door opened and the Earl came in.

She thought as he walked towards her that she had never seen a man look so happy.

He reached the bed and sat down on it facing her.

"Is this true or am I dreaming?" he asked.

"It is — true," she whispered.

He looked at her for a long time without speaking until she said,

"You are – making me – feel shy."

"I adore you when you are shy!"

He did not kiss her as she expected.

He took off his robe and climbed into the bed beside her.

Then he pulled her into his arms and she felt her heart beating frantically against his.

Because he was so silent she asked after a moment,

"What – are you thinking – is there anything wrong?"

"How could anything be wrong now that you are my wife?" he said. "I just want to go on thanking God for having sent you to me and it is still difficult to believe that the problems, the loneliness and the misery of the last years are really over."

"I vowed that I would – make you – happy," Jaela murmured.

"And I vowed, my darling little wife, that I would never lose you."

Then, as if he was afraid that he might do so, he held her closer still.

Next he kissed her until it was difficult for her to breathe.

"I love you," he said when he raised his head. "But, my precious, because you are so very young and I know very innocent, I would not hurt or frighten you."

Jaela put out her fingers to trace the line of his lips.

"You are never to speak of either of us being frightened again," she said. "Because of what we have suffered, I know that there is only one thing that can destroy fear and keep it from hurting us."

"I think I know the answer," the Earl said, "but tell me."

"It is Love," Jaela replied, "and I love you with – all my heart and – with all my soul."

"As I love you!" the Earl said, "and I also adore your beautiful body. Will you give me that as well?"

"It is – yours for always!"

There was a little note of passion in her voice that he had not heard before.

Then she whispered a little hesitatingly,

"You have said – you think – me clever – but you know I am – very ignorant about – love."

She drew in her breath.

"Suppose you are disappointed – and you find me dull – and I bore you – "

The Earl knew that this was an important question.

"My darling, my sweet," he replied, "do you think I want you to know anything about love except what I teach you?"

He pulled her almost roughly against him.

"You are mine and no other man shall ever touch you."

His lips then took possession of hers as if he was afraid that he might lose her.

Then, as the Earl kissed her and carried on kissing her, he knew that, when he awakened her to the ecstasy of love, it would be the most thrilling and exciting thing that he had ever done in his life.

He would be very gentle and they would both know the irresistible rapture of desire that would carry them towards the stars.

It would be the real Love that came from God and was part of the Divine.

It was the Love against which nothing evil and nothing that was wicked could survive.

He felt Jaela quiver against him and drew her even closer.

"You are mine, my precious, innocent little wife and I will love you and worship you for the rest of our lives."

"I-I love you," Jaela whispered. "I believe you are — lifting me — up to Heaven — and the angels — are waiting for us."

Then, as the Earl made her his, they were both enveloped with the Light of Love, which comes from God, is part of God, and is Eternal.

OTHER BOOKS IN THIS SERIES

The Barbara Cartland Eternal Collection is the unique opportunity to collect all five hundred of the timeless beautiful romantic novels written by the world's most celebrated and enduring romantic author.

Named the Eternal Collection because Barbara's inspiring stories of pure love, just the same as love itself, the books will be published on the internet at the rate of four titles per month until all five hundred are available.

The Eternal Collection, classic pure romance available worldwide for all time.

Made in the USA
Columbia, SC
19 January 2022

54475433R00119